MURDER IN THE SHAWANGUNKS
•
CLASS OF '68

Ward Eastman mysteries
by Norman J. Van Valkenburgh

Murder in the Shawangunks
Mischief in the Catskills
Mayhem in the Catskills
Murder in the Catskills

MURDER IN THE SHAWANGUNKS

A Ward Eastman Mystery

by Norman J. Van Valkenburgh

CLASS OF '68

A Mountain Top Mystery

by Airilee Ellyn Blessing

PURPLE MOUNTAIN PRESS

Fleischmanns, New York

Murder in the Shawangunks and Class of '68
First Edition
1999

Published by
PURPLE MOUNTAIN PRESS, LTD.
1060 Main Street, P.O. Box E3
Fleischmanns, New York 12430-0378
914-254-4062
914-254-4476 (fax)
Purple@catskill.net
http://www.catskill.net/purple

ISBN 1-930098-01-4
Library of Congress Catalog Card Number:
99-076006

MURDER IN THE SHAWANGUNKS

I

I N THIS PART OF THE COUNTRY, Ward Eastman sometimes felt
out of his element. Or, maybe, he was a little homesick. This was
one of those times.

The climb through the talus, here consisting of blocks of Shawangunk grit ranging to boxcar size, would have been a tough scramble
for a younger man. For someone in his early 70s, it was a major
contest. It hadn't helped matters when folks down at the research
center asked him to keep an eye out for rattlesnakes. It wasn't said as
a warning; rather, it was pure science. They had been keeping track
of a den near here and wondered how this year's young were doing.
He hadn't seen any snakes—and was thankful for that—but when
the round, brown, fallen tree limb moved underfoot and scraped
against a rock, he jumped higher than he'd been able to in years. It
was hot, too, and waves of heat reflecting from the rock's surface
made it seem hotter than it really was. It all added up to a confirma-
tion of an early translation of the Dutch word Shawangunk as
meaning "the place on a very bad hill."

He had found signs of the old boundary line even though trees
were few and far between. That any trees at all grew in this chaos was
a testament to the proficiency and persistence of nature. The blazes
on the trees were put there by Carmer all right; his inverted V mark
was distinct.

Eventually, Eastman reached the footpath running along the base of Near Trapps, the cliff that soared 100 feet and more overhead. While the line climbed it, he had no intention of doing so. It looked sheer and smooth, but he didn't doubt some agile and daring climber had found a route up years ago and probably had given it one of those odd names first ascentionists felt was their right and responsibility.

The footpath ran in both directions along the bottom of the cliff. He followed it southwesterly to where it ended at what was probably the final climbers' route on this end of Near Trapps. A bushwhack took him to Smede's Cove, a break in the escarpment where he could make his way to the top of the ridge and the Millbrook Ridge Trail that followed it. He turned northeasterly and walked the trail. Finding open slabs off to one side, Ward selected what looked like a comfortable rock (none really were) and settled on it, leaning his back against the gnarled pitch pine that grew conveniently next to it.

It was still hot, but the shade of the tree and the gentle wind dusting the ridge cooled things to a comfortable level. The smoke from his pipe dispersed quickly, carried off the way he had come by the northerly breeze. The air was clear and the broad sweep of the Catskills filled the horizon facing him. He could see the Indian Head Range far to the northeast. The distant hills swept around—Plateau, Hunter, West Kill, Balsam, and beyond to Ashokan High Peak, which was almost due north on his compass. Slide and the great peaks that looked up at this highest mountain in the Catskills were blocked from view by the imposing hulk of Dickie Barre looming on the far side of the Coxing Kill. These faraway peaks marked out his career in a wide panorama. He had climbed them all at one time or another but, as the years passed, they grew higher and higher and the climbs took him longer and longer. Retirement hadn't come easy. When he reached the magical age of 70, he hadn't much choice but to accept it.

After muddling through a year of idleness and growing ornerier by the day (at least, that's what Betty, his wife, kept telling him), he decided he wasn't built for that kind of life. When word of his pending retirement got around, the people down at the Preserve had approached him about coming to work there on a part-time basis.

"You set your own schedule; come and go as you like," they said, but he had declined. He had lots of projects planned he told them---fishing, hiking, putting his survey records in order---all important things he had put off for too long. However, that make-work stuff hadn't been as enjoyable or rewarding as he had imagined and after a year or so of feigning contentment, he asked the Preserve if the offer still held. It did. That had been over two years ago.

The Preserve amounted to over 6,000 acres, most of which had been parted off the vast resort property, known as Trapps Mountain House, that covered most of the ridge and had been amassed by three or four generations of the Miller family starting back in the late 1800s. It had become too vast for one entity to manage so it was split into two parts. The hotel and ancillary buildings and facilities constituting the resort occupied about 2,000 acres in the center of the original tract. This was surrounded by the Preserve, which was managed as a membership organization with the lands being open to the public on a fee basis. Extensive research was conducted at the Preserve into environmental relationships between plants, animals, rock, habitat, weather, etc. and had been ongoing for nearly a century. The storehouse of information gathered in the process was considered by those who knew about such things as the best and most comprehensive in the eastern part of the country. Educational programs drawing students from local schools were conducted by a staff of educators well-versed in natural history.

No matter how valuable the Preserve and its reason for being, its objectives and programs depended, at least in part, on knowing what lands it owned and where its boundary lines were. One would have thought those so concerned about acquiring the many lands making up the total property would also have made sure they knew where each parcel began and ended. At the time of the purchases, much of the ridge was open land used as pasture by the valley farms. Quarries dotted the landscape and here the Shawangunk grit was blasted from the solid rock to be fashioned into grindstones and huge blocks used in foundations for buildings around the countryside. They also provided the basic material raised by master stonemasons into the sprawling, multi-storied hotel that perched on a ledge overlooking the cold, clear waters of a tarn that formed the centerpiece of the resort.

In those days, everyone knew who owned what and surveys weren't really necessary as the land changed hands, usually being handed down from one generation to the next. In time, however, this knowledge faded as the old folks died and their offspring sought escape from the hardscrabble life by moving to the hopeful bounty waiting in the surrounding villages.

So it came to pass, in the late 1930s, the Millers realized the time had come when the property had to be surveyed and the boundary lines marked out on the ground. By then, clearings had filled in with trees. Where hay fields once ripened into second cuttings, forests held sway and waves of timothy stalks no longer rippled in the breeze. Glens and cul-de-sacs hidden within jumbles of fallen rocks and ledges seemed deeper and darker as the hemlocks there grew to gigantic proportions. Stone walls that once marked pastures and meadows disappeared beneath the thick growth of the ubiquitous laurel, its only value being the vibrant pinks and whites of the plants' late spring blossoms that drew visitors to the resort. The local gentry had long ago discounted the usefulness of this plant by observing it was too coarse for hog feed and not big enough for fence posts or firewood.

Roy Carmer (Actually his first name was Royal, but that regal name was used only by his mother. All others knew him by the shortened version.) had been a summer visitor to the resort for a number of years. He lived in Pennsylvania and came to the ridge for the month of August each season to escape the oppressive heat of his home country. A much-respected surveyor, his profession was also his hobby. Even during his vacation, he spent his time wandering the widespread lands of the resort seeking out old property corners and remnants of long-forgotten rail fences and hedgerows. He was a familiar sight to hikers along the miles of foot trails that criss-crossed the property. Some thought him a bit eccentric; he never used the trails and was often seen standing on the tops of moss-covered ledges, a folded map in hand, sighting to some distant object with a large, brass compass he carried in a leather case hung by a strap around his neck.

It wasn't surprising then, in August of 1937, when Carmer was approached by the Millers with a proposal to contract with him to survey the outbounds and interior parcel lines of the overall resort property. Both knew it was a long-term project and might require Carmer to relocate his home and business. It didn't come to that however. A deal was struck whereby the research, field work, and mapping of the survey would be carried out in the warm weather months of May through October during which time Carmer would be provided board at the hotel and residence in one of the small cottages nearby. The remainder of the year he would be free to return to Pennsylvania and operate his business there. His crew for the summer work would consist of men hired locally.

The survey progressed. Each summer saw a few miles of the outbounds run, cleared, and blazed with corners set. These consisted of 1½" pipes with a cap stamped with numbers noting the year it was set. In places where ledge rock prevented the driving of these pipes into the ground, piles of stones were built. No shortage of these existed; the ridge was strewn with rocks of all sizes left by retreating glaciers millennia ago and the detritus remaining from the stone cutters' work. Interior parcel lines were run, but not marked. Roads, buildings, streams, outcroppings of rock, cliff lines, and any other physical feature that didn't move was tied in. A single map was planned to illustrate the overall picture of the property. It was added to each year and kept current with the field work. It would be bed-sheet size when completed; the border measured 5′ by 12′. By the end of the summer of 1941, it looked like one more season would see both the survey and the map finished.

However, events in 1941 conspired to bring the project to an early close. The first was a tragic thing. Isaiah Denning, one of the local men hired for the survey, fell from the high cliffs on Dickie Barre and was killed instantly when he struck the talus rocks below. He had been alone at the time, at work setting piles of stones at angle points in the boundary line which ran, according to the old deeds, "along the top of the high rocks facing the Coxing Kill." It was late in the season, around the first part of October, and the shock and grief of it all pretty much put an end to the field work for that year.

About the same time, a couple of the fires set by the berry pickers down the ridge got away from them. They burned for days despite valiant efforts by local volunteer fire companies, forest rangers, fire wardens, and men from CCC camps brought in from all parts of the state. It had been a dry summer and the pickers should have known better than to be setting fires, but it had long been a common practice and supposedly improved the crop in following years. To make it that much worse, the biggest fire was on Millbrook, a part of the resort property, where the berry pickers weren't supposed to be to start with.

Of course, December 7, 1941, was the "date that will live in infamy." Why that affected the completion (or, more accurately, the non-completion) of the survey may not seem readily apparent, but it did. Roy Carmer enlisted in the army the next day, fought the war in Europe, moved to California when it was over, and never came back to the Shawangunks.

The survey was halted in mid-stream so to speak. The unfinished map was carefully rolled on a wooden pole and placed in a specially-built tube, which was sealed and stored in the archives up in Oak Cottage where most of the Miller family papers were kept. The many deeds Carmer had laboriously copied by hand in the vault of the county clerk's office in Kingston were numbered, indexed, and boxed. Carmer's meticulously annotated field books were gathered together, put in order, and locked in a glass-fronted bookcase. In the end, the story of the survey, not yet fully told, took up one corner of an anteroom next to the archives office. There it rested, moldering (much like John Brown's body) and waiting for some future surveyor to pick it up and see it through.

2

THE LONGER he sat there, the more Ward Eastman came to accept that closing his career out on the survey line in the Shawangunks wasn't really that bad after all. The ridge lines weren't as high as those in the Catskills although they were a lot steeper. And it was interesting to be working in land patents that ran back to Colonial times and earlier. He had heard of the Groote Transport, the Nineteen Partner Patent, and other early allotments, but hadn't known much about them. Tracing the work of a previous surveyor was easier than trying to keep up with the younger men (and, occasionally, women) of today's survey crews. He could still swing a mean ax, but the new generation had adopted machetes as the tool of choice, and he was too set in his ways to make a switch this late in life. When he needed help dragging the chain through the woods or running a transit line, Lars Robertson, the Preserve's ranger/naturalist, helped. He was as old as Ward, and their pace was a close match. So it all worked out.

The records of Carmer's earlier work were so thorough, it was almost like being there with him. The transit Ward used was the one Carmer himself had used although it actually went back to a prior era. It was an 1898 K&E and weighed a ton. It could still accurately turn angles and the sensitive, sweeping needle of the compass was a gem.

It was Carmer's field notes that set his work apart. Kept in a neat hand, they recorded every feature he encountered along the line. The distance to stream crossings was carefully noted as well as the bearing of the flow. Ledges were recorded in detailed sketches; heights of land were tied in when they were topped; trails, woods roads, stone walls, remains of rail fences, hedgerows, were all noted by bearing and distance. The date and weather were recorded at the top of each right-hand page of the field book along with the names of the men on the crew for that day and the task assigned to each—axman, transit man, rear chainman, etc. When a corner was set (usually some time after the original traverse), a description of it was written in the margin as well as the date and the initials of the person who set it. Sometimes this was in another style, indicating Carmer wasn't always the one who put the corner in place.

When he retrieved the records from Oak Cottage and moved them to the room assigned to him at the research center, Ward spent a few days sifting through the material to see what he had. The old, wooden, four-drawer filing cabinets held folder after folder of deeds, letters, hand-written notes, and other odds and ends of papers. Each folder had a number corresponding to a parcel of land of that same number on the bed-sheet of a map. Almost everything one needed to know about the parcel was in the folder.

It was the photographs, however, that really surprised Ward. In the glass-fronted bookcase where the field books were kept, he found a long row of small brown envelopes on the shelf beneath the books. Each envelope held photographs of corners—capped iron pipes, piles of stones, Xs cut in ledge rock, etc—and was numbered and dated. With no index or other key, it took Ward a few minutes before he was able to match the photographs to the field books. As it turned out, the numbers on the envelopes related to the numbers of the field books and pages within them. Thus, envelope C-16-20 referred to the corners set as recorded on pages 16 through 20 in Field Book C. More than one photograph had been taken of some corners. These were from different perspectives, taking in some distinctive background feature—a large round boulder, an oddly-shaped tree, the profile of a ledge, the view of a distant ridge, and so on. With these in hand,

Ward had been able to reestablish missing corners by orienting them to the features depicted in the photographs.

Taking all this together, Ward soon found that picking up the "tracks" of surveyor Royal Carmer was an enjoyable and rewarding experience. If only some of the lines he was following didn't run through chain after chain of impenetrable laurel. Or over rattlesnake dens.

The bottom drawer of one of the wooden cabinets held a miscellany of files. Some appeared to be personnel files of individuals who had worked with Carmer on the survey. These included pay records, work assignments and, in a couple of cases, obituaries and other items clipped from newspapers. Some contained lists of equipment and supplies used on the survey and others held information on local events including forest fires that had occurred on or near the hotel/resort property. The thickest one covered the 1941 fire and included a number of newspaper items that told the story of the fire from beginning to end.

It had been a big fire and Ward leafed through the papers out of curiosity after accompanying staff from the research center to the site where a continuing study was still being conducted to track the succession of plants and animals following the fire. Over time, many of the markers outlining the fire's perimeter had disappeared and Ward had been asked to replace them. This hadn't been too difficult because Carmer had drawn a map of the fire area a few days after it had been extinguished.

It hadn't been the first forest fire on the ridge, nor the last by any means. It probably wasn't the biggest either but had obviously captured the attention of the local newspapers and their readers. That might have been because this was one time when it was certain the fire—fires actually—had been set. *The Ellenville Journal* reported four separate fires were burning at one time and "a can containing kerosene and rags" had been found at the point where forest rangers determined one of the fires had started. This had been on the Trapps Mountain House property and was, evidently, the site Ward and the researchers reconnoitered.

Although the arsonists hadn't been identified, it was apparent the fires had been set by huckleberry pickers who spent the season in camps all along the ridge while harvesting the berries and selling them to buyers in Ellenville. It had been a dry summer, the berry crop hadn't measured up to that of previous years, and scrub pine and pin oak were taking over some of the best patches. When this happened, about the only way to improve conditions was to clear the land by fire. Bumper crops usually followed in a couple of years. This had been done, so the newspaper said, but the fires got away in the dry conditions and the pickers couldn't control them.

It took nearly a week to put out the fires. The blazes spread quickly over the parched ground and through the dry forests. Surface fires dropped over the edge of cliffs and became crown fires as trees beneath them ignited. Ground fires moved under rocks and smoldered for days in deep crevices. Fire fighters came from all over. CCC camps from faraway sent crews. Inmates from the state prison at Napanoch were trucked to the fire line and formed into teams closely watched by armed guards. State forest rangers and fire wardens directed the operation and were somehow able to bring a modicum of organization to the motley group of individuals available to them.

Not surprisingly, the first smokes were reported by the observer on the fire tower at High Point on Ice Caves Mountain. His log recorded the sighting at 2:17 PM on October 2. Of particular interest to Ward Eastman was the final paragraph in the first *Journal* story. Roy Carmer, surveyor for the Trapps Mountain House, had been working on boundary lines in the far northeasterly reaches of the resort land, reported the newspaper. Finishing his work in the late afternoon, he had taken a route over Bonticou Crag. From the open summit rocks he had seen billows of smoke rising some distance away. From his vantage point he couldn't be sure of the source of the smoke, his view southerly being blocked by Guyot Hill. However, it appeared the smoke came from the vicinity of the hotel and he feared it was on fire. He had rushed off the Crag and down the carriage road to where he had left his truck in the morning. As he rounded the hill, he was relieved to see the smoke was some distance beyond the hotel. On reaching his office, he learned about the fires burning on Millbrook. Carmer and a number of the men who worked with him then joined the fire fighters and stayed on the line throughout the duration of the fire.

Since clippings from later years weren't included in the file, Ward couldn't help wondering how much the fire had improved the huckleberry crop, if at all. However, maybe berry picking was drastically curtailed during the long war years that followed, and it didn't matter one way or another.

3

WARD EASTMAN snapped out of his reverie. He hadn't fallen asleep, but nearly so. The warmth of the sun combined with fatigue brought on by the tiring climb up the ridge had made him more than a little drowsy. His pipe had gone out long ago. Without looking at his watch, he gauged the lateness of the hour by the angle of the sun. He had a long walk back to where he had parked his truck at the lower end of the line. However, it was all downhill.

The Millbrook Ridge Trail dropped over open slabs and through scattered pitch pines to the relatively level ground at the steel bridge crossing the state highway. Here he found Tim, the chief ranger on the Preserve staff, who had evidently been waiting for him to appear.

"I wondered if maybe you were taking a nap up there."

"No," Ward answered, "but I did take a longer rest than usual. These old bones don't recover as quickly as they once did. What's the problem?"

"Come on, I'll give you a ride back to your truck. I left a ranger there in case you decided to come down the line instead of out the trail. I'll fill you in as we go along."

The story had been brought in by the ranger who was patrolling out in the northeasterly end of the Preserve. He had heard chain saws along the abandoned section of Canaan Road. Dropping off the ridge to see what was going on, he found a crew of loggers cutting the trees in an area next to the road. In talking to the loggers, he learned they had a contract to timber the lands of the hunting club that stretched all the way from Springtown Road to the Preserve boundary high on the ridge. No, they hadn't bothered with a survey, the club's caretaker said it wasn't necessary; he knew where the common boundary line was. That was news to Tim and his rangers. That had been one of the lines they never had been able to locate—not just with certainty, but not at all.

"It sounds like those loggers aren't going to wait for anyone to sort out boundary lines. Once they get a log deck built and landings cleared, they plan to start working on the Old Mountain Road to put it in shape to hold trucks. You know that road; it runs over the ridge next to Canaan Road, across the wet area, and up the far ridge where the Preserve land is—or where we think it is anyway."

"Yeah, I know the road. It joins the one that runs northeast out of Spring Farm and past Table Rock," Ward acknowledged. "I haven't done any work on the lines up there."

"Well, guess it's time. I can give you a ranger or two to help out."

"I'll pull some maps and deeds when I get back to the research center. I'll drop into the county clerk's office tomorrow morning and see what I can dig up there. Give me a few days to wander around the ridge. Carmer must have put in lines. Maybe I can find them after I check his records and get on the ground. When I need help, I'll let you know."

The Northern Preserve, as this area was known (even though it was as far east as north), was pretty much of a no-man's land. Trails reached into it and along the Old Mountain Road. Hikers didn't visit it since the hike out and back had to be over the same trail because loop trails hadn't been put in. Deer hunters did frequent it in the fall, but most of these came in from the adjoining private land, especially from the hunting club down on Springtown Road. Rangers weren't able to collect user fees from those they ran into out there because they weren't sure where the Preserve land began and ended.

Even Roy Carmer had given it short shrift. He had covered most of the rest of the Preserve, but had evidently saved this for last. His bed-sheet map showed some boundary lines, but these had been plotted from deeds or aerial photographs. Bearings, distances, and corner descriptions were few and far between. Old roads were accurately plotted as were stone walls branching from them. Two of the old field books included road traverses dated early in Carmer's tenure indicating he had done this work as a base for the survey and map. Ward knew from the file on the 1941 forest fires that Carmer had been working on the ridge when he spotted the fire on Millbrook. However, he hadn't returned after that, leaving behind a blank on the map, so to speak.

The deed files weren't of much help. The deeds under which the land had been acquired by the Miller family back around the turn of the century were there all right, but most of the descriptions cited only adjoiner names and provided few bearings, distances, or any other specific calls. Fortunately, Carmer's field books gave some help or, at least, one of them did. Field Book L was the last one. Dated the months of August and September of 1941, this field book included notes of the survey of the line along the land now owned by the hunting club. The crew listed was R. Carmer, chief of party and transitman; A. Van Huelvan and L. Wynkoop, axmen and chain. The notes had been kept by Carmer—Ward was well familiar with his precise, neat hand. He was relieved to see marginal notes describing the corners that had been set. These were dated "10/2/41" and initialed "RMC." Ward realized these were corners set by Carmer on the day the forest fires had started and must have been what he was working on when he had spotted the rising smokes over Guyot Hill.

However, Ward didn't find the usual envelope of photographs of these corners. He went through the row of them one by one. He had previously checked the envelopes to be sure they were in order and carefully replaced each one he took out when working on a boundary line. The last envelope was labelled L, but the page numbers were prior to those of the Northern Preserve work. Must be, Ward concluded, Carmer had gone to war before getting back on the ground to take the usual round of photography. Well, he'd have to get along without pictures and rely on the field notes.

The trip to the county clerk's office helped some. A couple deeds to adjoining properties described corners as being "stones around a chestnut sapling," and "a pile of stones near the top of a hill," and

other distinct and permanent monumentation. At least, more permanent than the point of beginning of one of the townships along the
Hudson River—"Beginning at a point marked by an X cut on the ice
in the middle of the Hudson River," read that description as Ward
remembered it. And certainly not as nebulous as a deed he had run
into while researching for a survey in Rensselaer County. The
property in that one began "at the left hind leg of the red heifer now
standing in the barnyard."

Ward drove the road that went past the buildings of Spring Farm
and through the fields beyond. The road then turned right and
followed an old lane between two stone walls through the woods. At
the far side of the second open field after that, the road continued a
short distance into another patch of woods and then was abruptly
blocked by a gate. He parked the truck in a pull-out next to the gate.
He still had some distance to go, but it would have to be on foot. Just
past the gate, the woods road joined the Old Mountain Road, which
led on for nearly a mile to the northeast before leaving the Preserve.
Here Ward knew there was another gate at a stone wall marking the
Preserve boundary line not far from Table Rock. The 1941 notes in
Carmer's Field Book L began at this point and Ward intended to do
the same.

The trail (or Old Mountain Road) dropped down a long hill at
the bottom of which stone foundations marked the homestead of a
one-time farm. The trail leveled out and tracked through a stand of
hardwoods. What had once been open pasture land followed with
stone walls running this way and that delineating one farm lot from
another. The trail then ran through a grove of hemlocks before
reaching the gate.

Carmer's notes ran a traverse southeasterly along the wall. Ward
took the bearing of it with his compass and found it only 2° off that
observed in 1941, that difference being the declination in the intervening years. While Ward had brought a chain along, he left it coiled.
The notes were complete with distances along the wall for over 15
chains where it ended. He saw no need to remeasure the wall for this
reconnaissance, which was simply for the purpose of locating corners
and angle points he confidently expected to find.

The field notes led the way up a short rise and then down a long slope shaded by gigantic maple trees. The wall crossed a stream—at 5 chains 40 links recorded the notes—and climbed steeply beyond that. For another 10 chains the wall tracked up one shelf after another, first a steep climb and then a short level stretch before another steep climb and so on. The wall ended at the foot of a long slope that appeared to run to the top of a ridge.

Ward snapped the coil of the chain into a figure eight and laid it out full length on the ground. The first corner was another 3 chains and 50 links beyond the end of wall. He wasn't going to measure this distance with any degree of accuracy. However, by tying the leather thong on one end of the chain to a stake and pulling it out along the bearing of the wall, this kind of rough measurement would indicate when he came near where the corner should be. This meant, of course, he would have to walk back to untie the thong and climb back to the front end of the chain, thus traveling each length three times.

Carmer's marginal note said he had "set pile of stones on steep side hill," but when Ward reached the distance, he found no such corner. He knew he hadn't made an error in tallying the number of chains for the relatively short distance he had climbed from the end of the wall and was sure his compass bearing had correctly produced the line. As rough as his method had been, Ward felt he was no more than 10 feet off. Still, no pile of stones proved him right. A number of stones lay scattered about the hill side, but these seemed to be there naturally and were not the remains of a pile destroyed by some animal or an irate adjoining land owner as sometimes happened. Examining all the trees within a 25-foot radius, he looked for Carmer's inverted V mark, but saw none.

Perplexed, Ward turned on the bearing of the next line, adjusting for the 2° declination indicated by his reading on the stone wall below. This line ran about right angles to the left for a distance of 5 chains and 15 links said the field notes. Using the same rough tactics as before, Ward laid out the line across the steep slope through a stand of mixed maples and hemlocks heading for, he hoped, "a stone set on end with stones piled around" as stated in Carmer's marginal note of

"10/2/41." It wasn't there and neither was Carmer's signature mark on the trees surrounding the point where Ward's traverse brought him. More than enough stones to build a substantial corner were scattered about, but these lay where nature, not man, had put them.

The deed to the adjoining property, which repeated a description from a deed written in 1842, called for the next corner to be "stones set around a chestnut sapling." This was confirmed by Carmer's notes; saying there he had found "a ring of stones around the remains of a large chestnut tree." He recorded in the margin that he had driven "a capped iron pipe stamped 1941" in the center of the ring of stones on "10/2/41."

The boundary turned right and climbed the last slope of the ridge. Measuring as he went, Ward topped the ridge at about 4 chains——the field notes had it at 3 chains and 90 links. In a small hollow another 2 chains farther on, Ward found the corner. The chestnut was long gone, taken by the blight in the early part of the century. The "remains" Carmer had found in 1941 had rotted further. All left now were a few pieces of decaying wood extending out of the ground from roots hidden in the duff. However, there was no mistaking the ring of stones circling the root mass. These had lain flat when first put down around the sapling in the early 1800s, but had been tipped up by the expanding girth of the tree as it grew and had remained that way when the tree died and decayed. Here was the corner all right, but no capped iron pipe marked Carmer's passing that way. Two nearby hemlock trees offered opportunity for his distinctive mark, but they were silent too.

It was time for a smoke and the contemplation that went with it. A fallen ash tree provided a convenient seat. Once the ritual of filling and lighting his pipe was complete, Ward spread out the deed copies he had brought and reread them comparing each with the sketch map he had drawn a few days before. He did the same with a copy of the 1941 field notes. Both records indicated without question he was in the right place. Carmer and his crew of A. Van Huelvan and L. Wynkoop had obviously been here too. But, then what? Carmer had come back a month or so later, but what had happened to the corners he had set? And why?

Ward Eastman had no answer to those conundrums. If a solution was to be found, it would have to come later. The problem of the present was to find the line of the hunting club property and that was still a long way off, over another ridge and beyond.

The deeds from here on wouldn't be of much help, most of their calls were for adjoiners only. However, Carmer and his crew had found stone walls in the lower elevations along with a few piles of stones, and the remains of a rail fence higher up.

His pipe out by this time, Ward folded the deeds and put them back in the front pouch on his pack. He put the old field notes in his shirt pocket for ready reference after setting the next bearing on his compass. He dispensed with measuring this line because about 10 chains along and down the slope of the ridge just beyond the old chestnut, Carmer had run onto a stone wall and had followed it to the bottom. Moving ahead on bearing, Ward noticed a line of large maple trees just after starting the down slope and followed these to where they reached the wall. The wall took him to the foot of the ridge and an old woods road. Here Carmer had turned right to run the centerline of the road for nearly 20 chains to where another stone wall crossed it. This wall marked the hunting club line and Ward turned right to run it up to the bottom of a line of steep slab rocks. Unable to climb these directly, he detoured to the left to gain the Old Mountain Road that snaked a tortuous course between the rocks to finally reach the crest of the ridge.

At this point Ward was pretty much lost as far as boundary lines went. The valley before him ran southwesterly to end against a line of cliffs about a mile away. The Preserve/club line crossed the valley in production of the last stone wall below the slabs, but no walls marked any line in this dead-end valley. Carmer's notes said he had found no evidence of boundary line or corners either, but had returned in October to set them. By this time, Ward knew he would find no corners no matter what the field book said. The only answer was to survey the lines he had walked that day and all those that lay ahead. Thinking about it, the first thing that came into his mind was the need to lug that heavy K&E transit up and down these hills, rocks, and ledges.

As it turned out, Tim assigned two of his rangers to the survey and it was they----young lads both----who carried the transit wherever it was needed. It was a long haul, the field work took them well over a month. Ward spent nearly two weeks on the computations and figuring where to set the missing corners. That and blazing the final lines took a further two weeks. Even at that, they were ahead of the loggers and forestalled any trespass on the Preserve lands.

Every time they set a corner----or reset it if one was to believe the annotations in the margins of Field Book L----Ward searched the site for some sign of Carmer's earlier work. A pile of stones here, a witness mark there, an inverted V blaze here----they found none. It was a puzzle wrapped in an enigma.

4

THE SURVEY, from the first field reconnaissance to the final blaze on the last tree, ran the calendar through the rest of the summer and darned near through the fall. At the beginning, the hills were tinged with the deep green—almost black—of summer. When it ended, the green had yielded to the browns, oranges, reds, and yellows of fall and these, too, had faded. The tops of the ridges were devoid of color except where the spruces, hemlocks, pines, and cedars stood out starkly against the barren landscape. High cliffs and low ones, too, traced gray lines across the hills. Snow hadn't yet dusted the tops of Guyot Hill, Dickie Barre, Millbrook, and the other summits, but cold nights harbingered its coming.

This was the time of year Ward Eastman moved indoors. On those days when cold winds blew down the valley, it was good to watch them stir the tree branches from out the window over his drafting table. On the pleasant days, which became fewer and fewer, he took care of odds and ends of field work yet to be completed. A few corners always remained to be set and some brushed-out lines still had to be blazed. By and large, however, this was the season he did the computations, drew maps, and wrote reports of surveys and boundary lines he had worked on earlier in the year. It was also when he researched the Preserve's and Carmer's records and the deeds on file up in the clerk's office in Kingston in preparation for next year when the snows of winter had melted and swelling buds and singing birds heralded the advent of spring.

He had put off one pressing boundary line problem for the last couple of years, but could avoid it no longer. About five years earlier, the state had acquired an extensive tract of land adjoining and southerly of the Preserve. This had been designated a State Park Preserve and was administered locally by a manager and staff, who took their policy directions from an Albany hierarchy, who probably didn't know a tree from a rose bush and thought all open space should be paved or covered with concrete block buildings. That unit of state government had recently reinvented itself as the Office of Parks, Recreation, and Historic Preservation, which sounded more than a little pretentious. Knowing a bit about government bureaucrats, Ward thought their interest in preservation was more apt to be that of preserving their own existence and high salaries.

Anyway, the state had acquired this tract of land and then had it surveyed by a private firm from down the Hudson Valley. That survey disagreed with Carmer's survey of the common boundary line between the two properties. In fact, the park's survey had created an overlap of about 10 chains along the line running from the Coxing Kill to the summit ridge of Dickie Barre. The whole thing hinged on the location of the division line between Lots 2 and 3 of the Groote Transport, an ancient and far-reaching patent of land created by the Trustees of the Town of Rochester in 1730. Over time, many lines of the 24 lots in the patent had been lost to antiquity. Current surveyors had to rely on remnants of old stone walls in an attempt to recreate the intentions of the early patentees. The park surveyors had picked up lines of stone rows in the southern reaches of the tract and had based their interpretations on them. Carmer had relied on stone rows in the northern part of the tract and, as the saying goes—or went—"never the twain shall meet." And they didn't.

The notes of Carmer's survey were in Field Book K. As Ward Eastman leafed through it, he noticed a few pages and the book's cover were stained with rust-colored spots. Noting the crew names listed at the top of the right-hand pages and especially the initials in the margin of the last few pages, he realized this was the book Isaiah

Denning had when he fell from the cliffs of Dickie Barre. This piqued Ward's interest, and he pulled Denning's personnel file from the bottom drawer of one of the wooden cabinets.

The file held Denning's obituary and a number of newspaper clippings. Putting these in chronological order, Ward was able to reconstruct the tragedy.

Denning had been working alone on the Preserve boundary line that ran along the top of the Dickie Barre ridge. As told by the marginal notes in the field book, he had been setting corners at the angle points in this line. At each point, the notations reported: "Set pile of stones. ID 10/2/41." Eight corners had been put up by Denning and, although not stated, he had probably hacked witness marks on the trees around the corners and blazed trees on the lines between them. A good day's work, Ward thought and more so when one considered the rugged climb up and down the ridge. Only Denning hadn't made it all the way to the bottom.

Denning was a single man, said the obituary. One of those interviewed after his body was found said, "He was a confirmed bachelor, who never put up with no truck from women." He lived by himself in a rustic shack not far from Trapps Chapel down on the old turnpike across from the site of Abe Billingham's store (once, it had gone out of business long ago and now stood an abandoned relic of the past, said one paper).

This had been the same afternoon when the fires on Millbrook and farther down the ridge had been set. Every man within a 10-mile radius was fully engaged in combat against them day in and day out after that. It was some time before anyone had missed Denning. On October 6, during a break from the fire line, Carmer had asked the men on his crew if they knew where Denning was. When they realized he hadn't been at the fire, two of the men went to his shack. He wasn't there, but casual housekeeper that he was, they couldn't tell when he last had been. Carmer and his men started a search along the traverse line they and Denning had put in from the Coxing up the Dickie Barre. Reaching the top, they found the corners Denning had set. They then fanned out and descended the ridge, searching for some sign of him as they went.

The upper part of the Dickie Barre is made up of a series of three ledges, each topped by a fairly level stretch of ground to the bottom of the next higher ledge. The top two ledges are known as Second and Third Dickie Barre. Only 20 to 30 feet high, these are easily climbed. The lower ledge, the First Dickie Barre, is a sheer cliff rising 70 or 80 feet and more with the base marked by a jumble of talus. Rocks as big as a car lay in confusion all along the lower slope. It was here they found Denning's battered body. They might have missed him, but one of men noticed red blotches on one of the rocks near the cliff. This turned out to be Denning's blood and marked the point of impact of the fall. His body lay on the far side of the rock. The men fashioned a makeshift stretcher from saplings, vines, and their own shirts and jackets and carried him off the ridge.

The next day Carmer, the local constable, and two state forest rangers climbed to the site where the body had been found. They retrieved some effects that hadn't been brought down the day before---Denning's ax, one of his shoes, cap, and the survey field book. They then climbed the cliff by a deer path that circled to the north and up through a gap in the rock wall. Turning southerly, they followed it along the top of the cliff to a point above where the body had been found. Here the path was at the very brink of the cliff with no trees or shrubbery between it and the edge. All agreed that Denning must have missed his footing---by slipping on a loose stone they surmised---and plunged to the rocks below.

The obituary said a service had been held in the Trapps Chapel with burial in the nearby Davis Cemetery. And that, mused Ward Eastman, spelled finis to the sad tale of the demise of Isaiah Denning.

The more Ward delved into the records of Carmer's surveys in Lots 1, 2, and 3 of the Groote Transport and the early deeds he ferreted out in the county clerk's office, the more he was sure Carmer had come up with the right location of the lot lines and the property lines that depended upon them. He had located stone walls lining an old road that led from the public road beside the Coxing Kill into what appeared to be the old Van Huelvan homestead and farm, the property acquired by the Millers back in the early 1900s and now a part of the Preserve. The bends in this old road matched the courses given in the 1840 deed that granted the right of way to the original Van Huelvan. The last 5 chains of the right-of-way were described as being "along the line between Lots 1&2 of the aforementioned tract." Using that as the line between those two lots, Carmer had found another stone wall 20 chains away (this being the width of Lot 2) running parallel to it and took this second wall as marking the line between Lots 2 and 3. The fact that Gus (for Augustus) Van Huelvan, a direct descendent of the original owners, had been on Carmer's crew at the time and confirmed the lines of the family farm clinched it as far as Ward was concerned. And, obviously, for Carmer too.

On the other hand, the park's map prepared by the contract surveyors accepted other stone walls that appeared equally substantial as evidence delineating lines between other lots of the Transport. Ward couldn't bring himself to believe a bunch of flatland surveyors from Rockland County had prevailed over Roy Carmer, who specialized in mountain and back-country surveys, but their determinations had merit.

To prove to himself which of the two was correct, Ward made more than one foray into the field that winter tracing the stone walls of each survey although some were partially hidden by drifts of snow. In the end, he concluded both surveys were correct. The park surveyors had the lot lines in the right place while Carmer had the correct lines for the original and extensive Van Huelvan farm. The conflict was created when the scrivener (probably an attorney, Ward concluded, who didn't know the difference between a tract lot line and the line between a sheep lot and a cow lot) of the first farm deeds described some stone walls as being lot lines when they weren't.

It was all worked out that winter between the park's people and those at the Preserve. They compromised and split the difference. Ward was directed to run a new line up the middle of the overlap. The two ownerships would then sign an agreement accepting this as the true division between the properties.

With the coming of spring, Ward was anxious to get on the ground. However, he held back until the sun had warmed enough to melt the sheets of ice coating the rock faces of the Dickie Barre ledges and cliffs. Finally, by mid-May, the way was clear. He decided to first

scout the Carmer line up the ridge and search for the corners set across
the top by the unlucky Denning. He found no envelope of photographs of these corners, but didn't really expect to. From what he
could tell from the files and records at hand, Carmer took the
photographs, not trusting any of his field men to do so. Since
Denning was alone that day, no photographs had been taken and,
considering the continuing battle with the fires, Carmer probably
hadn't found time to go back later.

It was an easy run---not the climb, but finding the old Carmer
line. Ward knew, from his winter treks, where the corner was at the
bottom and which stone wall marked the line. He followed this to
its upper end. Taking a bearing back down it with his compass, he
produced it on up the ridge. He picked up a few inverted V blazes
along the way and came eventually to the base of the First Dickie
Barre. The sheer face confronting him presented an insurmountable
obstacle. Recalling the newspaper account of the investigation of the
accident, he moved along the base of the cliff to the north. It was
rough going; huge blocks of talus forced a number of detours. He
assumed one of these marked the point of impact where Denning had
fallen, but had no way of knowing which one.

After a particularly rough scramble over one huge rock, he
picked up a game trail on the far side. This brought him to a cleft in
the cliff. He climbed the steep grade and turned southerly back along
the top of the cliff. He kept watch for some sign of Carmer's line
continuing uphill. At one point, a clump of pin oaks forced him and
the game trail out to the very lip of the cliff. Here must be where
Denning fell, Ward decided. The empty space below caused him to
reach for a tree, a bush, something, for support, but none was within
reach except for the pin oaks. These being replete with sharp barbs,
he was discouraged from using them as hand holds. This delicate
stretch of trail continued for about 30 feet with a single break. About
halfway, the pin oaks gave way at a couple of large, flat rocks. These
offered a convenient seat from which one could admire the sweeping
view from Sky Top all the way around to Millbrook and beyond.
However, the exposure of the spot only prompted Ward to hurry

along to where the trail left the edge of the cliff and moved in among some pitch pines.

After some backing and filling, Ward finally picked up Carmer's distinctive blaze on a large black oak. The compass bearing directed him onward and upward over the Second Dickie Barre and the Third to the top, where the most southerly of Denning's piles of stones greeted him.

Traversing northerly with the aid of a copy of the 1941 field notes and some inverted V blazes, Ward found the remaining seven piles of stones. Each was perched on the very edge of the low cliff that marked the high point of the Dickie Barre (originally called Stone House Bergh, as Ward had found it named in the early deeds).

The summit ridge was interspersed with open slabs of rock from one end to the other and presented even more sweeping views than those from the high cliff below. Ward was high enough now to see the Hudson River, the Berkshires of Massachusetts, and the Housatonic hills in the far distance.

The survey of the new division line was anticlimactic. The challenge had been figuring out who had earlier done what and why. That accomplished following days of searching out and reading often indecipherable deeds and untold hours spent tracking down tree blazes and forgotten stone walls, the rest was just plain bull work. Fortunately, as in other major surveys of Preserve lines, he was allotted a couple young and unsuspecting rangers to lug the heavy transit up and down the ridge and to wield dull machetes at the tangles of vines and laurel barring their way from time to time.

5

WARD EASTMAN couldn't quite understand what the God-awful rush was all about. Once the field work was completed, both the people at the Park and the Preserve wanted the map and description of the new line to be drawn as soon as possible---yesterday, in fact. Ward was also anxious to get the matter off his desk, so was happy to comply even though past experience told him that once the paperwork reached officials in Albany, the rush to judgement would give way to the slow pace of the bureaucratic maze. About this time, the newspaper article appeared.

The *Daily Freeman* in Kingston in cooperation with local historical societies all over the county had been printing a series of weekly articles on the heritage of various communities. These dealt with places, events, and people of the past. Many articles included interviews with old-timers (called senior citizens or golden-agers in the modern age, but old-timers to those who were) who recalled earlier times---the "good old days" to those who had forgotten what a hardscrabble life they had been born to. The interview with Gus Van Huelvan caught Ward's eye.

Although Gus didn't mention working on surveys with Roy Carmer, Ward felt sure he was the person listed as one of the crew in the field books and who had guided Carmer around the lines of the family farm back in 1941. He told the interviewer about his great-great grandfather owning a large piece of land over at the Trapps and that he still had a place there to go back to if he wanted. His family had been stone cutters who used "to make millstones from Shawangunk grit." He told about the lost gold mine over on Millbrook Mountain where a cave "goes way back in" and another "big cave, very much larger, on Dickabarr mountain." And snakes—"I'm not afraid of snakes I see. It's the snakes I don't see I'm afraid of."

The picture of Gus Van Huelvan that accompanied the article showed a hale and hearty individual who was living out his days in the so-called Residential Care Center at Golden Hill. A true country gentleman, he had dressed for the interview, wearing a white shirt and dark trousers held up by suspenders. He was clean shaven, his hair was neatly parted and combed—he appeared a dapper man.

Disappointed that neither Gus nor the interviewer had gotten to the subject of surveys in the late 1930s and early 1940s, Ward decided to conduct his own interview. He called the Golden Hill facility to see if he could visit Gus Van Huelvan and, if so, would he mind answering a few questions about his work on the survey crew. The pleasant receptionist called back the next day to say Gus would be happy to see Ward and arranged a time and date.

Ward thought to take some kind of gift for Gus and wondered just what would be suitable. He finally decided on a book telling *The Story of Trapps Mountain House* in a 1932 edition he located in a used-book store down in New Paltz. Besides being a narrative history of the place, it was filled with a number of photographs illustrating the growth of the resort over the years. Ward felt Gus might enjoy a reminiscence through those pages of the past.

When Ward arrived at Golden Hill on the appointed hour, he was directed to an open patio around back. Gus was waiting there taking the sun in a lawn chair. He was in the same trousers, suspenders, and white shirt, all spotlessly clean. He was, indeed, as dapper as the newspaper photograph had indicated. Ward introduced himself and offered his hand. Gus took it without rising, saying his knees didn't bend as good as they once did.

They talked first about the weather, as country folk are wont to do. With that bit of protocol out of the way, Ward explained who he was and that he was retracing the boundary lines Roy Carmer had put in some thirty-five and more years ago. "You worked with him on those surveys. I see your name listed in some of the old field books as an ax man and chain man."

"Yep. I was one of the crew. Not all the time mind you. There was a lot of us. We all had other things to do, stock to take care of, gardens to tend, wood to cut for winter, and all such. Besides, he warn't in the field all the time. He had numbers to work at, deeds to look up, maps to draw, and other things that took him inside. He didn't work at it all year long either. The pay was pretty good and that extra saw us through some long and cold winters."

"You must have had to do a lot of walking on those surveys."

"Not near as much as you'd think. Most of the old farm roads was open then. Not growed up like they are today. And we had Truck P——that's what they called it——to get around in. A 1929 Model A it was. It'd go most anywhere. It was kind of a station wagon sort of thing. Wood-paneled. No windows, but it did have side curtains which we never used rain or shine. Had seats for six, three rows of two with room left over for the transit and all the other parapher-nally. A neat rig, I'll say."

"What kind of a man was Carmer to work for? Was he a hard worker himself?"

"Wal, I don't say he was an easy man to work for. But he didn't ask anyone to do anything he wouldn't, so you'd have to say he was fair. He just had some funny ideas that most of us didn't take to."

"What do you mean by that?"

"Wal, you see he was a Mormon or a Pilgrim or something like that coming from off in Pennsylvania like he did."

"I think he was a Quaker," Ward gently corrected.

"Yeah, that's it. I never could keep those odd religions straight. Over in the mountains we was just church people or we weren't and didn't need no fancy names so others would recognize us. I wasn't near as churchy as the missus. She'd go up to Trapps Chapel nearly every Sunday, but I usually found something important that needed doin' right at that time. She was a good woman all right."

Gus looked at the sky for a moment. Ward thought he saw a glistening in the corner of his eye, but Gus shook his head and went on.

"That's how come old Roy got coming to the House in the first place, you see. He was dead set against drinkin'. Didn't set with his religion, he said. And they didn't serve no hard stuff up at the House back then. Maybe still don't for all I know. So old Roy hit it off right good up there. They was kindred souls or some such thing. Peas in a pod."

"Did he try to preach to the men who worked on his crews or did he accept you as you were? I don't suppose you drank, did you?" Ward asked with a smile.

Gus smiled back. "Wal, I'd take a nip now and then, that was kind of a tradition down in the Clove. We had to have something to warm us up on cold winter's evenings. We made our own, you know. Coin came dear and prices down at Fowler's Tavern were a bit more than we could handle. If we wanted a snort, we had to have our own brew or none at all."

"I saw your name in the field book of the survey off Old Mountain Road between Table Rock and the Canaan Road country. Do you remember that one?"

"Yep. That was a long one. We didn't have much luck findin' corners. Sometimes we weren't sure where we were. I couldn't cipher what the deeds said, but old Roy spent a lot of time readin' 'em over and over. He'd sit on a rock out there in the woods every few chains or so and pull them deeds out of his pack and add up and subtract and multiply the numbers in them. He'd send us off chainin' this way and that 'til we thought we was goin' in circles. I guess we was sometimes. But we run onto an old stone wall now and then and, by cracky, then old Roy would smile. He figured it all out in the end. He were a good surveyor. I'll give him that"

"Do you remember going back to set the corners and mark the boundary lines?"

"Nope, I don't recollect that. Hold on a minute though. Old Roy did that himself. He was out doin' that when those damn berry pickers set all those fires."

"What about the fires? Did you help on them? I read the old newspaper clippings in the files and they said the fires burned for days."

"Wal, they did that for sure. If it hadn't been for the rain, we'd still be out there, I suppose."

"Rain? They didn't mention that. Was it rain that finally put them out?"

"Yep. It had been about the driest year I ever remember. Hadn't rained for weeks. Months, actually. Everything was dry. Even the Coxing stopped running and that hadn't happened since Moses was a pup. When you walked through the woods, it sounded like you was steppin' on egg shells. Why those damn fool berry pickers decided that was the time to set a bunch of fires, I'll never know. They should have realized they'd get out of hand and they sure did."

"When did the rain start?" Ward asked.

"Oh, I don't rightly recall. A week or so after the fire started, I'd reckon. We had the big fire about out except for that burning down in the rocks and no way anyone could be sure all that was out. We was pretty well done in by then. Black as night we was, from all the soot and cinders. Looked like we'd been born that way. Wal, the rains came and washed us down and put out the fire. It rained and rained day after day like it would never stop. What had been dry dirt turned to mud. Rotted off half my taters and other stuff still in the garden. Cold, too. Didn't get to snow, but felt like it was comin'. Warn't fit for man or beast out in the woods."

"Did you get back on any surveys that fall?" Ward wanted to know.

"Wal, just one. Somebody up at the House who paid a mind to recording that sort of thing wanted a survey of the fire before old Roy headed back to Pennsylvania. So, he got a bunch of us together and we run a line around the outside of what the fire had burned. Took us three or four days. Rained most of the time we were at it. I guess old Roy drawed a map of it when he got home, but I never seen it."

"Yes, he did draw a map. We have it up at the research center. It was dated late in November. So, like you say, he must have drawn it at home and mailed it back to Millers. I haven't found any field book for the survey though."

"Wal, I don't know about field books. Old Roy usually took care of all that technical stuff. Anyway, that fire survey was the end of the season. Old Roy packed up and headed back to Pennsylvania. We never did see him again, what with the war and all."

"I've found a lot of Carmer's marks on the boundary lines I've worked on. These are mixed in with the usual blazes one expects to find. What's the reason for the mix?"

"Wal, there's three things old Roy never let any of us do. We couldn't run the transit. Of course, he didn't mind us carryin' it all over creation. We weren't allowed to touch that camera he carted around wherever we went. He done all the picture takin'. And we couldn't make that mark on the trees. That upside-down V was his signature he used to say and we wasn't allowed to use it. And we didn't." Here Gus stopped and chuckled to himself. "All except Ike, that is."

"Who's Ike?"

"Why, Ike Denning. Him what was killed up on the Dickabarr."

"I wanted to ask you about that, but first, why was Isaiah Denning, or Ike as you call him, allowed to blaze trees with Carmer's mark and the rest of you weren't?"

"Wal, he weren't allowed neither. But, you see, he and old Roy didn't get along none too good. Sometimes Ike would try to irritate him just for fun. Like with that mark. These two big hemlock trees growed out next to Ike's cabin. One day when he'd had more than his usual snort of tonic, he went out with his ax and put a whole lot of those upside-down Vs all over them two trees. When old Roy come by a few days later, he saw them marks and was sure some mad, let me tell you."

"What happened up there on the First Dickie Barre? Why do you think Denning fell?"

"Think? Warn't no think about it. We all knew why he fell. He was drunk, that's all, and walked right off the cliff."

"Are you sure?" Ward wondered. "I've read the newspaper articles about the accident and some other papers back at the center and don't remember anything like that."

"Wal, I don't suppose that kind of stuff gets in the papers. Leastwise, not back then. But that's the answer, and that's why Ike and old Roy didn't get along. I already told you we each made our own drink. Couldn't afford to buy it. Mostly it was just plain apple jack. Some made beer and that was pretty good, too. Ike now, he made his out of corn and, let me tell you, it had quite a jolt. I never drank kerosene, but I kinda think it would taste a lot like Ike's tonic. That's what he called it, tonic. 'Good for what ails you,' Ike used to say."

"Did Denning drink on the job? Is that why Carmer and he didn't get along?"

"Yep. That's it. Ike used to take a jar of it in his pack along with a sandwich and an apple or two. We all carried our own lunch. Ike had been in the army in the war—World War I, that is—and had this old pack left from his service. Brown it was, with a lot of straps and buckles to do it up with. After a while old Roy began to wonder how come Ike was gettin' drunk durin' the day. So he went through Ike's pack once when we was out front clearin' line and had left our packs back near the transit. He found the jar then. Empty it was. He chewed Ike out somethin' fierce. Every morning after when we started work, old Roy made Ike open his pack to see if he was carryin' any of the drink. If he was, old Roy made him leave it behind. That sure did upset Ike. He never cottoned to old Roy after that."

"I suppose when he worked alone he took his tonic along and that's what happened the day he fell," Ward suggested.

"Yep. Not much doubt about that. Usually old Roy didn't let Ike go in the woods by himself for just that reason. But on the job up on Dickabarr, Ike was the best located to do the work of clearin' line, settin' corners, and stuff one could do by himself. You see, he lived right across from the old Billingham store where a road ran from the old turnpike up and over the ridge. All Ike had to do was walk up the road and there he was, right where the work was."

"If Denning walked the road to get on the ridge, why didn't he walk it coming back down? When he fell, he seemed to be coming down the traverse line. How do you explain that?"

Here Gus chuckled again. "Probably to visit the widder woman who lived down near my place. Down near Split Rock. Folks tried to make somethin' out of Ike's stoppin' in there off and on, but warn't nothin' to it. She just used to cook him up a fittin' meal now and then. Lord knows he needed it. I told him more than once he couldn't live forever on hedgehogs, squirrels, and other wild stuff he caught. For all that, Ike was a good worker. We was all sad about his accident. Most of the folks in the Clove went to his service up in the chapel. He must have been surprised to look out his coffin to see us all spruced up and sittin' there in church."

About then a nurse came out on the patio as if looking for something. "There you are," she said. "If you don't get inside, you'll miss your supper."

"It's my fault," Ward responded. "We got talking about a lot of things and forgot the time. I'm sorry."

"Now, don't be sorry. They'll see I get fed," Gus said. "I'm glad you came and thankee for the book. I'll sure enjoy lookin' through it. Come back another time. I'm pretty easy to find. We haven't talked about half the stuff I remember."

"I'll do that," Ward agreed as Gus and the nurse made their way in through the door.

Ward walked around the building to where he had parked the truck. His mind churned over the stories Gus had told him. It would take some time to put it all together. It had been a long, but interesting, afternoon.

A few days later, when Ward and Carl Huff, the Preserve's director of research, happened to both be in the office, Ward asked if he could look over the weather records for October, 1941. By then, the research center and its predecessor had been recording the daily weather at the Trapps property for over seventy-five years and was recognized by the weather people in Washington as the longest, continuous-reporting weather station in the country. The records for years past were neatly filed in boxes stacked on metal shelves in the vast storeroom. Carl dug out the reports for 1941 and left Ward to leaf through them.

It was pretty bland stuff, of use only to those with an interest in weather and its changing patterns, but valuable nonetheless. The long sheet for each month had daily columns for maximum and minimum temperature and the range between the two; precipitation, both rainfall amount and snow depth with beginning and ending times for the event; wind direction; the character of the day; a summary sidebar where totals for the month were entered; and a place to record unusual or miscellaneous phenomena.

The spring and summer months before October recorded only traces of precipitation confirming Gus Van Huelvan's recollection. The rain started on October 10, over a week after the fires began. It rained 1.36 inches that day and nearly half-an-inch every day after that until October 23. The temperature dropped as much as the rain—on October 16, the high for the day was 41° and the low was 34°. The highest temperature during the whole two-week period was 51° on October 3. Indeed, as Gus had said, it "warn't fit for man or beast out in the woods."

6

HE SUMMER turned into fall and brought a new October. The hills—both the distant Catskills and the near Shawangunks—turned also, into a kaleidoscope of colors to mark the season of change. As usual, this display of nature's wonder beckoned people to the House the better to admire the scenery. Leaf-peekers they were derogatorily called by the locals who had watched this display for years becoming quite blase about the whole show and not really understanding what the fuss was all about. However, two of those stopping at the House were there for another reason.

A telephone call had come to the research center asking if the surveyor was in. Well, he wasn't, that being one of the two days each week he didn't work, but he'd be in tomorrow the callers were told. Could they arrange a time to meet with him then; they were staying only the week. After explaining they were the daughters of Royal Carmer, who had done surveys of the property some years ago, they were assured Mr. Eastman would be available the next day at their convenience. And he was.

The knock came on the door at exactly 10:00 AM, the appointed hour. Ward greeted the two neatly-dressed, genteel ladies in their mid-50s and welcomed them in. They seemed a bit taken aback to find a man of nearly their father's age filling the roll he once had held, but recovered quickly.

The usual amenities took the next hour or so. They were from California, where the family had moved after the war. Both parents had passed away a few years ago as had their own husbands. They were widows with time on their hands and had always wanted to visit the Trapps Mountain House. Their father had spoken about it and his work there so often. And here they were.

Ward took them on a tour of the center stopping last in his own office where he showed his guests their father's field books, files, and the old wooden cabinets. He set up the K&E transit on the lawn out front and explained how their father had used it to survey the boundary lines of the property. He spread out the bedsheet map and they all marvelled at the size and workmanship of it.

As the visit concluded, the ladies said they had brought a box of things their father had kept when he sold his business together with the equipment that went with it some years before his death. Not knowing what else to do with it, they had thought a good repository would be at the Preserve, the location of one of the surveys he was most proud of. Ward walked the ladies to their car and accepted the box with thanks. Their mission accomplished, they returned up the hill to the House.

Ward carried the box to his desk. Opening it, he found it contained a thick packet of papers consisting of sketch maps, deed plottings, and correspondence relating to various land parcels now owned by the Preserve. And, Field Book M. Leafing through it, Ward saw that it included notes for only the traverse around the perimeter of the fire on Millbrook. The dates on the right-hand pages were late in October of 1941 and, sure enough, A. Van Huelvan was listed as one of the men on the crew. The weather each day of the field work was the same, "Rain. Cold." The box also held a number of books; a 1927 edition of Breed and Hosmer's *Principles and Practice of Surveying*, a 1925 edition of Cary's *Manual for Northern Woodsmen*, a 1929 edition of Tracy's *Exercises in Surveying*, a 1930 edition of Skelton's *The Legal Elements of Boundaries and Adjacent Properties*, Vega's *Logarithms*, Benson's *Natural Trigonometric Functions*, and other texts, all tools of the trade, so to speak. A leather case with a frayed strap held a large brass compass fitted for attachment to a Jacob's-staff. At the very bottom of the box was a camera.

This was shaped like a flat box about 9 inches by 4 inches and a couple of inches thick. Ward had seen cameras like that years ago, but not recently. The front opened and folded out to a 90° angle. It had a metal track along the inside surface on which the lens, view finder, and shutter, all affixed to a bellows, slid out. Ward pulled out the bellows. The dry fabric split as he slid it into place. It hadn't been used in years and, now, would be never again. He slid it back and closed the front of the camera. Turning it over, he opened the cover on the back where film was loaded and was surprised to see a film wound on the take-up spindle. He quickly snapped the cover shut to keep out the light and sat there holding the camera in his hands.

Had the film been used, he asked himself? If so, considering the state of the bellows, it must have been long ago. What were the photographs of? Could the film still be developed? Being a neophyte when it came to cameras, he had no idea of the probable answers to those questions. Not trusting himself to handle the camera further, he put it in his briefcase.

The young man staffing the counter at the shop in New Paltz said he had never seen a camera like that before, but was sure his father, the owner of the store, had. The father, who came out from the back room, indeed remembered when cameras such as this were among the best available. He opened the back and removed the film. Yes, it seemed in good condition, he said as he turned it over in his hands and yes, he thought it could be developed. It might take a week or so, because they would have to send it away for processing.

In less then a week Ward heard from the shop telling him his pictures were back and could be called for anytime. Having been full of speculation since leaving the film, he waited no longer. After picking up the envelope of prints he stopped at the deli next door, bought a tall lemonade, and took a seat at one of the little tables out front. He looked at the pictures one by one in the order taken. They were black and white, which was not surprising considering the probable vintage of the film.

The first picture was of a pile of stones. Ward didn't immediately recognize it, but did when he looked at the second picture. This was of the same pile of stones, but from a different angle. It was the northerly of the eight corners along the summit ridge of Dickie Barre. The following three pictures were of the next corner south. The next was of the succeeding corner and on it went down the ridge until each corner had been depicted in at least one photograph.

The pictures of the fifth and sixth corners showed more than piles of stones. Off to one side, Ward noticed a small canvas pack festooned with many straps and buckles. Surely this was the World War I pack carried by Isaiah Denning when he was in the field. It certainly fit the description related to him by Gus Van Huelvan.

What was the story behind the photographs? Gus had said Carmer allowed none of the men to use the camera. Certainly, from what Gus had described as the relationship between the two, Carmer wouldn't have let Denning even handle the camera much less take a photograph with it. But Carmer, on the day Denning was setting corners on Dickie Barre, was in the Northern Preserve setting those corners——the ones Ward hadn't been able to find. The only answer seemed to be that Van Huelvan and the newspapers had the wrong date for the time Denning was setting these corners. If that was true, then the annotations in the margins of the field book were also wrong. That seemed unlikely given how particular Carmer was about keeping accurate notes and records.

The supposition of the wrong date was put to rest by one of the photographs of the eighth or most southerly pile of stones. The background of this photo was to the southwest over the open slab rocks to the distant Millbrook Mountain. There could be seen a spiraling plume of smoke rising from the trees at exactly the point where that fire had been set. In the foreground of the picture sat the old canvas pack leaning against the base rocks of the large pile that had, it appeared, just been built.

The final two pictures in the old roll of film suggested a story Ward was reluctant to read even though it was one he had suspected for some time. He recognized the location. The view was along the edge of the cliff at the top of the First Dickie Barre. It looked toward the two large flat rocks at the center of the 30-foot stretch where the game trail walked the brink. The pin oaks grew on the left and the open cliff loomed on the right. A man was in the center of the first picture; his head was tilted back and he was drinking from a wide-mouth Mason jar.

The next photograph was taken from the same point as the one before and the view was the same. The man was leaning over the rocks and putting the now-capped jar into a battered canvas pack with a number of straps and buckles on the sides and top.

And that was the last photograph on the old film.

7

THE CALENDAR cycled over to November with its frosty mornings, crisp days, and clear nights. The leaves had all fallen except for the withered and leathery few still held by the oaks. They could be forgiven that oversight because they dropped bushels of acorns in late September and early October.

It was a long shot. Ward Eastman knew that. Still, he had to give it a try. He pulled the truck into the little grassy area next to the Coxing and retrieved the pack from the box in the back. He had bought it at the Army-Navy Store in Kingston; they hadn't been able to find one from World War I, but had dug out a beat-up, olive-drab pack from the next war, the big one. It had straps and buckles that nearly matched those of the pack in the old photographs taken on Dickie Barre. Ward had packed it with a pint plastic jug of lemonade, a sandwich, two apples, an old shirt, and some odds and ends comparable to what Gus Van Huelvan had said Ike Denning usually carried. It did look about the same bulk as the one in the photographs Ward thought as he slung it on his back.

He took the now-familiar traverse up the ridge easily following Carmer's marks. The line steepened and eventually brought him to the base of the First Dickie Barre. He turned to the north and followed the game trail to the gap in the cliff face. He scrambled up and moved back south to stop at the two flat rocks where the trail skirted the top of cliff. He laid the pack on one of the rocks. Opening the front flap, he took out the roll of red flagging he had picked up at the hardware store that morning. He pulled off a number of 3-foot lengths of the flagging and tied these to the buckles on the pack.

He looked over the edge of the cliff to the jumble of talus below. On the right, a huge oak tree reached for the sky. Next to it, the hulk of a long-dead pine reared like a skeleton, its barren limbs spreading every which way. Ward was sure both trees had been there in 1941. Smaller pines and oaks swept around to the north leaving an open space only on the left. The rocks here were piled in confusion, covering the slope so that acorns and seeds, no matter how determined, couldn't find enough soil to set down roots.

Facing in that direction, Ward took the pack in one hand and threw it as hard as he could. It tumbled over and over with the red flagging streaming out behind. It landed with a thud on top of a great sloping rock and then rolled over the far edge of it. He marked the spot in his mind and reversed his route back to the bottom of the cliff. Clambering with difficulty over the large rocks, he reached the point where the pack, now scuffed and torn open along one side, lay beside the rock it had hit on its downward flight.

Using this as the center, Ward ranged round and round in ever-increasing circles. He looked under rocks, big and small, and scraped away the leaves, twigs, and limbs that had gathered in the cracks and hollows of the jumble. He found nothing, only nature's odds and ends rewarded his search. Oh, well, he hadn't given much hope for it anyway.

The climb and the effort of swarming over, under, and around the huge blocks of Shawangunk conglomerate had been tiring. He returned to the pack and sat on a flat rock out in the open where the sun now warmed the chilly air of the morning. He pulled his pipe from his pocket, carefully tamped the bowl full of tobacco, and lit it. The sun moved on its journey across the sky casting shadows that danced in the rocky chaos where he sat. Something sparkled beneath a large, canted rock some way in front of him. It seemed as if one ray of the low autumn sun had simply reached under the rock and picked out a crystal to rest upon. Ward was sure that's what it was—a fragment of quartz imbedded in the rock, but he went to look anyway.

It wasn't a rock crystal. It was, instead, a shard of blue glass. Its luster had faded, but enough remained to catch the sun and reflect it. He carefully moved the rock fragments covering it and found a circular piece still screwed into a tarnished zinc lid with a milk glass seal inside. It was the remains of the top of a one-pint perfect Mason jar. He dug further and saw more fragments of the blue-point glass, three rusted and discolored buckles, a rotted shred of webbing, and a small, battered and rusty metal box. With his jackknife, Ward pried open the box and found that it held a few coins. Ward scraped at their corroded surfaces and rubbed them against the sleeve of his shirt. He was barely able to make out the dates—1936, 1939, 1936, 1940, 1941; none newer than that.

He left all of it where it lay and returned to his seat on the rock. It was clear now; this only confirmed what he had already concluded. It was the icing on the cake, as the old saying goes. He could picture that day in his mind.

On October 2 long ago, Royal Carmer and Isaiah Denning put in the line Ward had climbed that morning. They blazed the trees as they went—Carmer with his distinctive inverted V and Denning with the standard blaze. Reaching the top, they walked to the northeasterly end of the ridge. Working their way back, Denning and, perhaps, both of them at times, set the eight piles of stones. Denning carried the field book and made notes in it as each corner was set. Carmer followed behind, taking photographs of each corner and blazing the trees between them. At the last corner, they saw the smoke from the fire over on Millbrook and hurried down the mountain.

For some reason or, maybe, by design, Denning got out ahead. He stopped at the two flat rocks and, Ward surmised, collected the Mason jar filled with tonic he had stashed there another time. Carmer came up just as Denning drained the jar and was putting it in his pack. After taking the photographs of Denning, Carmer confronted and berated him for not abiding by the rules of the survey. Whether Denning fell in the scuffle that followed or was pushed by an irate

Carmer, who completely lost his temper, no one would ever know for sure. But Ward, considering the facts he now had at hand, favored the latter.

Carmer then took Denning's pack and hurled it into the wide-open space beneath the cliff. It landed next to the slanting rock far from where Denning's body lay. There it remained, disintegrating and disappearing with the seasons and time. Being well off the beaten path, no one had passed that way since. Until today, that is.

Carmer hastened down the ridge, passing Denning's mangled and lifeless body as he went. Arriving at the research center, he gave out the story of seeing the smoke from Millbrook as he topped Bonticou Crag. Later, in a quiet moment between stints on the fire line, he annotated Field Book L with descriptions of the corners he planned to set on the Northern Preserve boundaries and dated them October 2 to fix an alibi should one be needed. Then, the rains and foul weather came and persisted. In addition, he was sent out to survey the perimeter of the Millbrook fire, all of which prevented him from doing the corner work. He returned to Pennsylvania on his usual schedule planning, no doubt, to set the corners when he returned the following spring. But, "the mills of God grind slowly, yet they grind exceedingly small" and Pearl Harbor changed the course of history and Carmer's plans.

Ward knocked the cold ashes from his pipe. He went back to the meager remains of Denning's pack. He moved the rock fragments back on top of them. He took some larger stones from nearby and wrestled them into place over the spot. He covered it all with leaves and dead limbs. To display this bit of the past for all to see would serve no good purpose, he thought.

He picked up the olive-drab World War II pack and slung it on his back. He moved through the maze of rocks and took the downhill trail.

CLASS OF '68

The Class of '57

Tommy's sellin' used cars, Nancy's fixin' hair,
Harvey runs a grocery store and Marjorie doesn't care.

Jerry's drivin' truck for Sears and Charlotte's on the make,
and Paul sells life insurance and part-time real estate.

Helen is a hostess, Frank works at the mill,
Janet teaches grade school and probably always will.

Bob works for the city and Jack's in lab research,
and Peggy plays organ at the Presbyterian Church.

And the Class of '57 had its dreams.
We all thought we'd change the world with our great works
and deeds, or maybe we just thought the world would change
to fit our needs.
The Class of '57 had its dreams.

Betty runs a trailer park, Jan sells Tupperware,
Randy's on an insane ward, Mary's on welfare.

Charlie took a job with Ford, Joe took Freddie's wife,
Charlotte took a millionaire and Freddie took his life.

Johnnie's big in cattle, Ray is deep in debt.
Where Mavis finally wound up, is anybody's bet.

Linda married Sonny, Brenda married me,
and the class of all of us is just part of history.

And the Class of '57 had its dreams,
but livin' life day to day is never like it seems.
Things get complicated when you get past eighteen,
but the Class of '57 had its dreams.

Ah, the Class of '57 had its dreams.

PROLOGUE

I LIVED my first eighteen years in Mountain Water, a tiny hamlet nestled in the Catskill Mountains of what people down in the city call upper New York State. When I became old enough to reason things out by myself, I decided the place got its name from a combination of the mountains circling it and the streams of water cascading down their steep slopes—especially in the spring when the deep snows high up seemed to melt all at once.

It was my grandmother who set me straight, as she did most everyone else regardless of the subject being discussed at the moment. She was correcting my father about one thing or another up until she died at the age of seventy-five and he was in his fifties.

She drove the mail route up the dead-end valley branching off the state highway that ran—probably as fast as it could—past the general store and post office centered in the circle of houses and farms that made up the village. Not far from the post office and set back from the road was a large, round cistern about the size of a small swimming pool, although I wasn't sure about the sizes of swimming pools since nobody in the village could afford one. It consisted of a wall of stones laid up to a height of about 3 feet with the inside lined with concrete. A long pipe extended out from the steep, rocky bank behind it and ran a steady stream of the clearest, coldest water I ever tasted, then and since. It splashed into the pool below raising a misty spray all around. During the hot days of summer, the kids in the village congregated there to be cooled by the spray and to frolic in the icy water that flowed over the edge of the wall and down into the creek that ran alongside the road.

One of the happiest memories of my growing-up years is riding the mail route with my grandmother—and my brother too, after he got old enough to come along without crying as soon as we got out of sight of our house. We stopped in the pull-off next to the spring on the way up the valley to read the post cards we would be delivering to mail boxes along the route and on the way back to read those being sent out. On one of these stops she told the story of the spring and how the first cistern had been built by the original settlers to store the water so it could be used by the families who made their homes nearby. They had named the community Mountain Water in honor of the spring that supplied them with one necessity of life regardless of season and in dry times and wet. It never once ceased to flow. After I learned to read, we no longer stopped at spring; instead, I sat on the floor by the front seat of the car and read the post cards aloud to my grandmother as she passed them to me, one by one.

As I look back on those days with the wisdom of maturity, I believe most folks on the route knew we were reading some of their mail. They never complained. In fact, they probably chuckled to themselves now and then knowing all about it while my grandmother and I—oh, yes, and my brother too—thought it was our secret. I wouldn't be surprised if some of the crazy things they wrote (at least, we thought they were crazy) weren't true at all, but a joke being played on us. Aunt Jane and Uncle Eli must have shook their heads over some of the events their relatives in the valley wrote about. All that, however, was long ago.

The cistern and the spring are still there and pretty much the same unless one looks closely. The concrete is cracked here and there and a few stones have fallen from the outside wall. The present generation takes them and the mountains and streams, the trees and birds, and the seductive tranquility of the place for granted. I and many others- young and old alike—consider this little hamlet called Mountain Water one of the prettiest spots on Earth. While I was growing up there I felt—because of the natural beauty of our surroundings—we all lived charmed lives. Unfortunately, in a later time, I found out bad things can happen in beautiful places.

ONE

I UNDERWENT a profound mid-life crisis in 1993 and blamed—at least partially—Bill and Hillary Clinton. Up till then, I had been pretty satisfied with my life. While it's true I hadn't really accomplished everything I expected to, that hadn't really been a problem. I just hadn't gotten around to figuring out what it was I wanted to accomplish. I'd been busy, raising a family, running a business, housebreaking the dog, but that was kind of a holding pattern. It was simply a matter of time until I took off like a rocket and fulfilled my unlimited potential.

I was smart, got good grades in school; everyone had expected me to go out into the world and DO SOMETHING. When I was eighteen, I truly believed someday my name would be in a headline on the front page of *The New York Times;* maybe not the lead at the top, but certainly one of those on down the page. Then, one morning, I woke up and realized, "Oh my God, my life is half over and I still haven't made much of an impact on the world." On reflection, I realized that while I hadn't made an impact YET, I probably never would.

Right in the middle of all this, Bill and Hillary were elected president. Besides feeling sorry for myself, every time I picked up a copy of *Newsweek,* Bill Clinton looked out from the cover reminding me I was married to a man who was the same age as the President of the United States. I suppose if I had looked at things positively, this would have given me a feeling of empowerment when I realized that, hey, at long last, my generation was in charge; but, it didn't. The thing I kept thinking was, while Bill Clinton is in charge of the country, my husband is mostly in charge of deciding whether we go to Wendy's or Pizza Hut on Friday night, and I wasn't in charge of anything. Unlike Hillary no one ever thought I infringed on my husband's decision-making prerogatives.

The problem was I had taken all that 1960s rhetoric a little more seriously than it was meant to be. No, a lot more seriously. I honestly thought we were going to be different. None of us was going to grow up to be part of the establishment. We weren't going to become a middle-class, materialistic society whose values were screwed up and didn't account for things that really mattered. We were going to forge a great new world in which everyone was graded equally and where the haves shared with the have-nots. Instead, we got Rolex watches, big cars, and hot tubs.

I thought my generation was a lot more altruistic than we actually were. Considering the way the '80s turned out, it's not surprising I had a mid-life crisis and got a little depressed. The surprise is I didn't blow my brains out.

The thing that's so aggravating about all this is I keep preaching to my daughter, Emma, how important it is to decide what you want to do in life and then go out and do it. My problem is I'm still trying to decide what it is I want to do.

Don't think I'm dissatisfied with my life because I'm not. That's what's so upsetting. I kind of like my life. I live in a house that's too big, too old, and has too many things wrong with it that we can't afford to fix, but it's an unusual house with a personality, and I like it. My husband is a nice man who is never going to be President of the United States or even president of his company, but he's a great guy and I enjoy having him around. I have a nice kid who hasn't yet set the world on fire but, on the other hand she hasn't blown it up either. I have an interesting small business I enjoy running, a cute dog, and a fun car, but (hang on, the important part is coming up here) this isn't the life I expected to live.

I was one of those people others said had all kinds of potential. During the first twenty-five years of my life people kept telling me I was going to do wonderful things. Somewhere around the time I faced my big four-oh birthday, I found out one had to have more than potential. That became clear the day Emma asked, "Why didn't you ever really accomplish anything?" You can start out on potential, telling yourself and everyone else that, yes, I am going to law school, run for Congress, write a play, whatever. Somewhere in your late thirties, you suddenly realize it's a quick skip from having lots of potential to being past your prime. I could have accomplished a lot, should have accomplished a lot, but didn't. I found 1993 so depressing because that was the year I concluded it wasn't a case of not accomplishing anything YET, it was a case of not going to EVER.

It came as a rude awakening knowing I wasn't just sitting around pretending to be this middle-class housewife waiting for my real life to start. I had to face facts. This was my real life. When I looked at it honestly, I had to admit I was just an average person living an average life in an average town surrounded by average people, doing average things and that was probably going to be it for me. Maybe it wouldn't have bothered me so much except for Bill Clinton. In a way it seemed like he had gotten my job. I spent a while blaming him, which I guess was pretty much what everyone else in the United States was doing, except they were focusing on issues and I was focusing on my personal life.

Of course, that approach is the reason I didn't end up with the life I had expected in the first place. I started out to get that life; or, so I thought. I did something which seemed incredibly bold and far-sighted although many of those who graduated from high school in the late 1960s tried something similar and unconventional only to end up derailing their lives, just like I did. However, I felt like quite the maverick, boldly going where no woman had gone before when I told my parents I was going to take a year off to "find myself." I know now I was fooling myself, not them. When I said "finding myself," I really meant I was going to party like crazy and avoid all responsibility. At the time, though, I thought I would go out into the big, bold world and sort of discover the niche out there just waiting for me to come along to fill it. I would simply step into it to accomplish all manner of wonderful things and pretty soon the world would be beating a path to my door.

What actually happened was I drove off in my MG, while my mother stood in the driveway, saying, "You just can't leave without any destination. What if something happens to you?" I was sincerely hoping something would happen, although with a teenager of my own, I now realize what she meant was I would probably get kidnapped and murdered before I ever got out of Greene County. I, on the other hand, was expecting to discover myself, my life, my purpose, all in pretty short order.

I did start with no destination in mind, although I headed down I-95 because Washington, D. C., was in that direction and the only interesting place I had been to, ever, was Washington when we went there on our senior trip. The reason I didn't find myself was because I stopped and picked up a hitchhiker outside of Triangle, Virginia. He turned out to be my husband---eventually, that is---although at the time he was stationed at the Marine Corps base at Quantico, where, it turned out, he was just sort of hanging around waiting for the government to send him to his real destination---Vietnam.

What with falling in love and deciding to get married, although not without an incredible amount of conflict because I was, of course, morally opposed to the war in Vietnam, I somehow lost sight of my more distant goal of changing the world; or, of changing myself. All of a sudden real life intervened. The next thing I knew I was keeping house, paying bills, and worrying I would become a widow practically before I had much experience at being a wife.

The next thing I knew he was home from Vietnam and couldn't get far away from the military fast enough. Then, he was in college. Next, we were thinking of buying a house and having children. All at once, I was forty-three years old and Bill Clinton was President of the United States. I was the one thing I had dreaded becoming above all else, a person who looked, sounded, and thought much like my own mother.

To tell the truth, I went through a dreadful case of the blues. I just sort of dragged through life, getting up in the morning, getting

Emma off to school, going down to Cal's Corner and opening the doors, but not really caring whether or not anyone came through them, coming home, fixing something to eat, going to bed, and getting up in the morning to start the whole horrible process all over again. My life hadn't turned out anything like I had hoped and somehow I hadn't noticed until it was TOO LATE. My life was practically OVER. I was never going to accomplish ANYTHING, or do anything that MATTERED, and what was the point of GOING ON. And wasn't it funny, just a real hilarious joke? I had left a boring, little town in upstate New York and here I was in a boring, little town in Georgia? Ha, ha, well I guess it was a real failure festival there for awhile and I must have been a tremendous pain to live with. Just about the time everyone around had decided to throw me off a bridge, I woke up one morning and decided, "Well, that's the way it's going to be. It could be a whole lot worse but, for the most part, I'm pretty happy, so let's just get on with it." And that was the end of that. Although now and then, at least before the Whitewater and Paula Jones things, I continued to have those twinges every time I saw the Clintons on television or the cover of *Time*. I sort of felt a moral obligation to go through a few minutes of torturing myself by thinking that could have been me.

Well, yeah, it probably could have been, as I was reminded when I received the invitation to my twenty-fifth high school reunion. There it was one morning, nestled inside all the circulars and advertisements, cleverly disguised as just one more piece of junk mail. In fact, I did almost throw it away until I looked at the return address and wondered why anyone would be sending me something from Plainview High School which, by the way, was a pretty dumb name for a school so far from the plains that looked out on a bunch of mountains. It was way too late for them to change their minds about my diploma. So I opened the envelope and it turned out to be this invitation to a reunion, complete with all kinds of involved instructions about getting my RSVP in early so I wouldn't miss out on this fun-filled weekend where I would have several exciting opportunities to reminisce with old friends about the best years of our lives. Not only that, the thing came with a questionnaire (three pages yet!) with hundreds of blanks to fill in describing all my wonderful accomplishments and fabulous experiences.

As I might have expected, the newsletter accompanying the invitation listed the amazing achievements of some of my classmates. Naturally, the ones mentioned were those who really had accomplished something: the doctor who treated the rich and famous from a Sixth Avenue office, the lawyer who had prosecuted some mob kingpin, the Pulitzer Prize-winning photographer and the best-selling author. Of course, I already knew about the author, because she was one of my closest friends during those school years. Besides, when I was in the throes of post-partum depression an my first day home for the birthing center, I had had the dubious pleasure of seeing her promoting her latest book on Oprah.

But I did feel a bit nostalgic reading those names and thinking about how much I had enjoyed high school. I wondered what it would be like to once again see the people who had been so important during my thirteen years of school and growing up. Would they look the same? More importantly, would they think I did? That's probably why Roger and Emma both insisted I attend, although this may have been part of their plan to get me out of the house for awhile.

Of course, I didn't went to go. I didn't want to be reminded of my past accomplishments––or the lack thereof––much less spend an entire weekend in the company of people who would remember me as a shining star in high school. Not only that, I wasn't sure I wanted to torture myself further with any more comparisons to old classmates. Considering the fact that we came from one of the smallest high schools in the whole country, a lot of them really had done well for themselves. This is not say I wasn't happy for them and even proud of what they had done. I just didn't want to be asked the question, "So, what have you been doing with yourself all these years?"

"Ellyn, it'll be good for you. You need to get away," Roger prompted from the hall closet, where he sat looking through an old issue of *Mother Earth News*.

I had laid down the law insisting he go through the boxes of stuff (junk?) he had been saving all through our marriage. For twenty years, we had been moving boxes of clothes that no longer fit, broken telephones, a computer that had been obsolete since 1975, perfectly good coffee pots that had been replaced by the succeeding generations of brewing miracles, etc., etc., only because Roger couldn't bear to part with any of it. We finally made a deal, he could keep whatever he wanted, but he had to look at each and every item to make sure it really was important enough to save. In return, I promised not to comment on anything he decided to keep. It had been slow going, because everything seemed to have some redeeming value, especially the TRS 80 computer, which he described as a "relic, which would eventually reach antique status." Sort of the way I felt about myself just then.

"Why is it so important to keep this?" I asked, picking up an avocado wall phone with a dial face. It's not like the Smithsonian is looking for an example of this hideous taste we had in the '70s."

"Oh, wow, did this belong to you, Dad?" Emma asked, holding up a vest that appeared to be made from mouse fur. "I'll bet you looked just like that guy who used to be married to Cher."

"Sonny Bono," Roger answered. "Emma, don't you think your mama ought to go to her high school reunion?"

Emma slipped on the vest and picked up a magazine from one of the piles. "Listen to this; what a weird magazine. Did you really read stuff like this? Yeah, Mom, you should go. It'll be good for you and, plus, you're always telling me not to worry about what other people think. So what if you're not some big deal doctor or lawyer or Native American chief. It's not like your life has been a total waste. Look at us." She leaned her head over on Roger's shoulder as they grinned identical grins at me.

"Okay, okay," I said. "I'll think about it."

I did think about it, to the point where I called Jan, my very best friend from high school and discussed it with her. Once we started talking, my concerns seemed to melt away. The whole thing stopped sounding like torture and began to sound like fun.

"Oh, don't be silly," Jan said long distance, getting right to the point exactly the same as when we used to talk for hours almost every night. "I was just talking with Jamie Timmerman. Do you remember him? He's the mayor now. Most people call him James these days. He hopes the whole class will come no matter who they are and wherever they are."

"Jamie's the mayor?" Did I ever remember him. Good looking, athletic, loved to party. The one guy all the others wanted to be; the one every girl had a crush on. Mayor? I remember holding his head while he threw up in my mother's flower bed after too much Boone's Farm wine. It was a long reach picturing Jamie as a pillar of the community. On the other hand, that was something I just had to see. If Jamie could make it as mayor, anything was possible.

I filled out the questionnaire—all three pages—trying to be honest. I answered the question, "What is your greatest accomplishment?" with the truth, which is that I had a lovely, talented daughter, who was the joy of my life and someone I would consider a friend had we known each other under different circumstances. I skipped over the one about higher education since I had had none, unless you count learning how to be a Marine Corps wife, with all the mysteries that involves.

"What kind of work do you do?" I gathered this didn't mean cooking, laundry, car pooling, and washing the baseboards once a month. I thought about this for a long time before answering with the following. "I own and operate Cal's Corner, a small bookstore, which I have tried to make as comfortable as possible, because it serves as a gathering place for some highly-original minds and interesting people." I didn't mention it also doubled as a way station for battered women, teenagers skipping school, bored housewives, and retired people who liked to read and talk. Or, that some days, the alcove in the back served as a day-care center. This was where I kept the childrens' books and it wasn't unusual to see three or four or more preschoolers sprawled full length on the thick carpet I had laid down there and playing with blocks, dolls, trucks, and toy soldiers or taking a nap while their mothers made a quick trip to the store, the dentist, or the hairdressers. The store was filled with books, of course, but also with easy chairs and couches. The coffee pot was always full and so were my customers, because even if I forgot to pick up doughnuts, someone was sure to show up with something to nibble on. I also didn't mention that most months receipts just about covered expenses, that I drew a salary resembling slave wages, and the whole thing was possible only because of a small inheritance from my Aunt Cal; hence, the name in her honor.

The paperwork had to be returned posthaste along with the reservation fee and picture of myself and family. I managed to get everyone—including the dog, the cat, and the fish in the background, swimming around in its bowl—together for a group portrait. All that was left was to call the travel agent, figure out what clothes to pack, make sure Jan really and truly wanted a weekend house guest, which she did, she assured me, although she warned I would have to put up with her ridiculous schedule as the only physician in a small town.

I began to look forward to going.

TWO

I F I HAD ANY REMAINING DOUBTS about attending the reunion, they vanished the next day. Roger had finished rearranging the hall closet; that's really what his efforts turned out to be. Nothing much had been discarded, but by turning heaps into piles, he was able to get the door closed without leaning against it. Having gained some enthusiasm from that accomplishment, he had descended to the basement. Well, it wasn't so much his enthusiasm, it was the ultimatum I had laid down, "Start cleaning either the basement or the garage, it's your choice."

The garage was almost a misnomer. We still had room for one car, but all passengers had to get out before it was driven in. The driver could open his door, but only if the passenger side was pulled to within a couple of inches of the towers of boxes that filled that side of the garage. It wasn't that we were a later generation of the Collier brothers, we were simply savers, although neither of us was sure what we were saving most of the stuff (junk?) for. In fact, we would have been hard pressed to tell anyone what treasures were in the bottom tier of boxes. They must have held something not quite solid because they squshed out on all sides, but we weren't sure what it was.

Roger's voice floated up the basement stairs and through the open door into the kitchen where I stood staring into the freezer trying to decide whether to take out chicken to thaw for supper or wait and call for a pizza delivery when the time came. The decision had to be made quickly or Cal's Corner would have a late opening.

"Come on down here, El, you've got to see this."

See what, I wondered, grabbing my jacket as I started down the stairs. Pizza was obviously the choice for supper. At first, I couldn't find Roger—we had only one light bulb down there and that left some dark corners. "Over here," he called as I saw the waving beam of a flashlight beckoning me to the farthest corner behind the furnace and hot-water heater.

Roger sat on one box with another open in front of him holding a book in his hands. Silently, he closed the book and handed it to me. I needed only a glance to realize what it was. There was Lucy on the white front cover, clad in her usual outfit—a plain, red dress and red socks. Her mouth was opened wide yelling out the numbers "68." Yes, it was my yearbook, surfaced after all this time. I had remembered packing it before one of our moves, but had no idea into which box when we moved the next time.

"Why don't you take it upstairs. I'll go down and open the Corner. You come along later."

With that he was gone up the stairs. In a minute or two I heard the car start and back out the driveway. I went upstairs, poured another cup of coffee (my third that morning), and sat at the kitchen table. Did I really want to open that book? It was a bygone era, one that seemed to have taken place in another world with a cast of characters who were now mostly unfamiliar. Oh, well, I thought, maybe I should at least look at the pictures. Recalling faces and the names that went with them would be helpful when I got to the reunion and suddenly realized I didn't know anyone or, if I did recognize a face, it would be nice to be able to put a name with it.

The first few pages listed the credits and pictured the administration, staff, faculty, and, oh yes, the board of education. My father was in that last photograph, wearing those horrible horn-rimmed glasses and that ratty tweed jacket neither Mom nor I liked. At least, he had his tie pulled tight in a neat knot, instead of hanging loose and with the top of his dress shirt unbuttoned, which was the way he usually went around—if he wore a tie at all, that is. Many of these people had passed on since the pictures were taken. Some had died---Jan had kept me up-to-date when their obituaries appeared in the local weekly---others had moved to different schools or retired to faraway places, disappearing from Mountain Water and Plainview High forever.

All this obligatory introductory stuff was followed by the individual portraits of members of the class. Opposite each was a listing of their accomplishments---Fashion Show 2, 3; Junior Prom Court 3; Band 1, 2, 4; Basketball 3, 4; Library Club 1, 2, 3, 4; etc.---and a cute quotation we each had selected to describe our inner feelings. Oh, my, we were young and quite a group, as are all classes as they near graduation, full of those dreams of great works and deeds the Statlers sang about.

Jan (short for Janice) smiled out from the page, her eyes looked upward---at the sky? Into the future? Of all of us, her future had seemed the most secure. Her father was a second-generation doctor. The last of a dying breed, he made house calls till the day he retired from practice. That day was when Jan finally completed her internship and returned home to hang her shingle on the wrought-iron post out front where her father's and grandfather's had hung. She had been my absolute best friend from our first day at kindergarten, when both of us, terrified at the new world we were entering, sought a friendly face. We selected desks next to each other that morning and, for the remainder of our school years, were never much farther apart. She moved like a whirlwind then and still did, trying to keep up with a practice really demanding two or more doctors. On her desk was a copy of the devotional *Meditations For Women Who Do Too Much* although, she said, she didn't have time to read it. Jan had never married. "No one ever asked me," was her usual reply to those who asked why not.

During the last couple years of high school, most of us thought that if Jan did marry, it would be to Chris Rafferty. The two seemed to be a match and neither denied it. However, Jan went off to medical school and Chris "found" his true love was really Beth Rideout, who had been in the class ahead of us. That was a rocky road from the start and they parted two years later with no children, fortunately, resulting from their short marriage. Now, he and Jan were again "keeping company," as my Aunt Cal would have said, but that seemed about as far as it would go. Chris looked seriously straight ahead in his picture, which fit with what he ended up doing. He had been chief of the local police force—all five men of it—for the last decade and was still a straight shooter after all these years.

It was Jamie Timmerman who was the real surprise. Mayor Timmerman? No, it couldn't be. I knew he now ran the family hardware store on Main Street, but until Jan's call, I hadn't known he had branched out into politics. It was Jamie who had been the first—as far as the rest of us knew, anyway—to smoke a marijuana cigarette and this in the eighth grade. A "joint" he called it, and we didn't know what he was talking about. Yet, he was the All-American boy, if ever such a personification existed. He was on every sports team in the school and served as captain on most of them. He never chased the girls; he didn't have to, they chased him. But he drank too much, drove too fast, and hung out with the wrong bunch—they being kind of rejects from the streets of the big city sent north to spend summers in the pure air of the mountains with Aunt Jane and Uncle Bill. Now Jamie was mayor and, probably, a good one—he charmed everyone and could be a friend to all, even to those who never had one. Jamie didn't smile in his picture; instead, he seemed to be unaware of what was going on at the moment. Deep in thought, he was probably planning some stunt to pull on some unsuspecting soul.

I had kept up with the doings of Anna Buckley through an occasional article in the national press and by seeing her name credited to photographs appearing in the glossy magazines. The biggest news as far as she was concerned was the Pulitzer. She had been waiting at a corner bus stop next to a bank in San Francisco when a string of police cars slid silently to a halt in front of her. She quickly realized a bank robbery was in progress. Thinking only of that proverbial "shot of a lifetime," she sprinted through the door of the bank, slid belly-down across the floor, and snapped a series of pictures of the ensuing gun fight while bullets, coming from both directions, screamed over her head. I hadn't seen her for years, but

Jan had told me she was leading a fast life, too fast in Jan's estimation. Anna was overweight, had high blood pressure, and was on the verge of being an alcoholic. Jan was her doctor, but was unable to get Anna to turn into the slow lane. Still single, Anna seemed destined to remain that way till the end of her life, which might be sooner than later according to Jan.

David Solomon had left the mountains as soon as possible. Now he looked at them upriver from his Sixth Avenue office---well, not really, because the windows faced south. On the other hand, he could have gone down the hall to look north from the other side of the building, because his suite spanned the entire twelfth floor. His was the name on the directory in the lobby, but only a few of the patients who took the private elevator to the twelfth got to see David. He treated the "really" rich and famous; the plain rich and famous were assigned to one of the bevy of doctors scattered around the many consulting rooms that filled the rest of the floor. Plush was the word for it. I had never been there, but Jan had when in the city once to a convention. David had taken her on a grand tour of "his little place." "Huh," Jan said, "if that's little my office is a bread box." But neither of us begrudged David his success. He had been this meek little Jewish boy who was picked on by everyone. A broad smile lit up his face in the picture. He was obviously full of confidence in himself and had every right to be.

Other then Jan, my closest friend in high school had been Molly Cornwall. It was books that drew us together. We haunted the library and, for some reason, always reached for the same book at the same time, which was annoying at first. She had moved to town at the beginning of our freshman year and I was sure I wouldn't like her; however, after glaring at one another for weeks as we pulled the books we each wanted this way and that, we both burst out laughing. Mrs. Griffin peered over the top of her glasses, rapped her pencil sharply on the desk, and loudly shushed for silence. But we couldn't stop and bolted out into the hall, arm in arm. After that, we shared books, secrets, laughs, and tears and knew we could positively depend on the other no matter what. Now, her latest book was on the *Times* best-seller list and I had it prominently displayed in the front window of the Corner.

"Oh, my God, the Corner," I suddenly remembered. It was nearly noon. I had daydreamed the morning away. Still, Roger hadn't called and neither had anyone else, so things must have kept on an even keel. I had pages to go and memories to unlock—until or if the phone did ring, that is.

It was inevitable that Gary Grissom would become a lawyer. He was always quoting some Supreme Court justice or pointing out what law we were about to break when we planned some scheme or another. I had forgotten he actually had worn a pinstriped suit the day our graduation pictures were taken, but there he was. I suppose if he could somehow have gotten a judge's robe, he would have worn that. After law school and clerking for a judge in the city, he had moved up to the district attorney's office where he had prosecuted the head of one of the Mafia families. He made a name for himself, but decided to leave it there and return to the mountains. Now, he practiced law from an office next to his father's liquor store on Main Street, held the elected post of county legislator, and served on the boards of directors of two banks.

Speaking of the law, our class—as with all others, I suppose—had a couple who were on the other side of it or, at least, skated perilously close to the edge.

Rory Hale was one of these. In his younger days, he was the typical country boy. Freckles dotted his cheeks and speckled his nose; his red hair completed the picture one would have found illustrating an early edition of *Huckleberry Finn*. He even wore a beat-up, wide-brimmed, straw hat and knew all the best fishing holes. He was smart—always ready with the answer to any question posed by the teachers—and seemed destined for real success out in the big world. However, this was the '60s and temptation lurked around the corner, even in our small and remote (or so we thought) part of the world. It caught up with Rory (or he with it) after graduation. He did time on a conspiracy to distribute charge and returned home with a ponytail, a ring in one ear, togged out in black leather, and riding a motorcycle. He was still a sweet, thoughtful, county boy to those of us who remembered him back when (he had been one of the cub scouts in my mother's den), but shocked most of the local citizens when he and two friends opened up a storefront tattoo parlor directly across from Gary Grissom's law office on Main Street. As if that wasn't bad enough, his partners in this venture only made it worse—much worse.

Mack Lucenti wasn't a product of Plainview High. Thank God for that. Actually, no one knew just where he did originate beyond the fact he had been Rory's cell mate in prison. Mack also had a motorcycle and, of all things, a wife who rode one of those highhandle-bar street machines that literally roared its way into town the day they arrived. That woke up the chickens as C. W. McCall said when he started down Wolf Creek Pass. They made a scary-looking trio with Wing, Mack's wife, being the scariest of all. By that time, I was long away from Mountain Water but got a detailed account from Jan during a long telephone conversation as soon as she had literally shoved her last patient of the day out the office door.

"You'll never guess who breezed back into town today and who—or what—he brought with him," she started out.

Of course, I didn't, but had no chance to say so as she went on. "Rory Hale, that's who, riding this big, long motorcycle. And he's brought along his cell mate from prison. Or cell mates, I think, by the looks of the gun moll who completed the group. You know what they're going to do?"

I didn't have an answer for that either, but still couldn't get a word in. "Remember where the barber shop used to be across from the liquor store?" I did know about that but kept silent, knowing it didn't matter whether I did or not. "Well, it's been closed up for years. That's where they went. Rory had a key. I don't know if they bought the place or are just renting it or what. Where do you suppose he got the money for either? Or for the motorcycle? They're going to open up a tattoo parlor. The woman—or whatever she is—is the tattoo artist. Gary went over to welcome Rory back and says his two friends—friends, did you get that?—are covered with tattoos. Good night! What do you think about that?"

Finally getting a chance to talk, I thought about saying something inane like, "It will be good to have a new business in town," but decided to save that for another time. What I did say was just as bad. "Does Rory still have his freckles?"

"What?" exploded Jan. "Freckles? Is that all you have to say? Oh, sure, you're way off in another country almost. We're the ones who're going to have to live with this."

"Calm down," I suggested. "It may not be nearly as bad as you think. Rory was a nice, quiet boy. I'm sure he hasn't changed that much. Don't you remember all those talks the three of us used to have and how much fun he was? He was a good friend to both of us."

"Yeah, I know. I hope you're right."

That had been long ago and the tattoo parlor was still there. So were Mack and Wing. And Rory, too. All were still whizzing around town on their motorcycles. The local folks had adapted and learned to live with it and, in fact, hardly seemed to notice anymore. Even Jan had a good word to say about them now and then and, once, went so far as to say the parlor was a clean place and Wing was very careful and proficient in running her business.

While we had a few who had gone far afield to make a success of their lives, a goodly number of our classmates had stayed in the area, married, made a steady living, and raised children who now went to Plainview. Our roster read a lot like the Statlers' "The Class of '57." Johnny sold used cars––and new ones too––down at his father's Ford dealership. Janie was "fixin' hair" and otherwise running her own beauty shop. Dan was assistant manager at the local Grand Union and Dolly, his wife, really did care––obviously––they had seven children. Zeke didn't drive truck for Sears, but did drive a taxi and one of the school bus runs. Susie wasn't on the make and never was; she worked receptionist desk at Gary's law office. Stanley sold life insurance and real estate, not part of the time, but all the time. Sally was a hostess at Al's Restaurant; Larry didn't work at the mill, but at the lumber yard; Patty taught grade school and probably always would unless she ended up being principal, which was entirely possible. Michael didn't work for the city but did enlist in the U.S. Army soon after graduation and was now about ready to retire. Oscar was in some kind of research, but neither Jan nor I were quite sure what for. Bernie played organ at the Methodist Church and piano with his five-piece combo, which played the "old songs" and was much in demand all over the eastern part of the state. Chad wasn't big in cattle, but did run the family farm.

I didn't know about anyone on an insane ward, but a couple of our less-fortunate friends were on welfare. No one had married a millionaire or, if they had, were keeping it a secret. Eddie had taken his life and for one of the better reasons; his wife left town one night with a cross-country truck driver and never came back----even for the funeral. A few had strayed outside their marriage vows and one or two were deep in debt.

And, then, there was Syd. He and I had been an item the final three years at Plainview. It was a foregone conclusion we would marry within a year or two after school. Even our parents had accepted that as fact. It didn't happen, however. I had every intention of coming back and settling down to wedded bliss with Syd after taking that year off to "find myself." Although I didn't know it until a few years later, Syd also found someone else in that year. Now, he and his wife ran a travel agency in another state and were the parents of two sets of twins. When I heard that, I was kind of glad I had driven down I-95 to seek my fortune.

After leafing through the yearbook and remembering----as best I could----everyone pictured in it, I concluded we were pretty much a normal class. We didn't have elections for honors such as "Most Likely to Succeed" that year and it's just as well we didn't. We wouldn't have taken them seriously if we had. We would probably have come up with categories such as "Most Likely to be Found Dead in a Ditch from a Drug Overdose," little realizing some of us might have fulfilled such a prophecy, or come close.

THREE

WHEN FIRST I BEGAN PLANNING this major excursion, I thought about spending only the reunion weekend back in the mountains and overnighting with Jan, but the more I thought about it, I realized it would be good to also spend a few days with my mother. After all, I hadn't seen her for a year. We kept in constant touch with long (overly long, I sometimes thought when the monthly bill came) telephone conversations, but it was time we caught up on things in person.

My father had died suddenly with a heart attack three years previously and she had been alone in the rambling old farmhouse ever since. My brother and I had wondered what would ever become of her without my father around; however, we were pleasantly surprised. He was a rather domineering person and, although I don't think he or she meant it to be that way, my mother was always a bit in the background. We thought she might withdraw into herself and from the world around her, but she did just the opposite. The absolute surprise was when she decided to take driving lessons. My father had encouraged her to do that for years, but she demurred saying the way other people drove, she would be terrified to get behind the wheel and take off on her own. A few months after the funeral, she decided it just didn't make sense to sit in the house going nowhere when a perfectly good automobile was taking up space in the garage end of the barn and running up insurance premiums. Once she got her license, she volunteered for all sorts of civic activities and was never home. Teasing her, we suggested the next thing, she would have a boy friend and be contemplating marriage. "Oh, no," was her retort to that. "The last thing I need or want is another man."

When I called asking if she'd be home the week following the reunion, her answer was a cautious, "Yes, but not all the time."

Once we worked it out that I would stay with her for the week, she closed our visit with, "I hope you're going to rent a car. I'll be needing mine." I assured her I was planning on doing just that and thought to myself, "My, how times have changed" and knew my brother would enjoy a rundown of that conversation.

It was good to hear my mother talk about her busy life. How she managed it all and still took care of that huge, huge, old house was beyond me. She did, however. Everything in it sparkled and always smelled so clean, which it was. We had moved into that house just a week or two before my brother's thirteenth birthday. I remember that so vividly because we celebrated the event with a party in the spacious cellar. The last I had been there, the walls still held the birthday messages we had painted with blue paint on the concrete walls.

My parents had purchased the 3-acre property, which included a barn as well as the house, for a number of reasons, so we were told in later years. One of these was the expansive lawn—just the thing, my father said, to keep my brother occupied should he ever complain about nothing to do. "And you, young lady, help your mother with the vacuuming and be sure to make your bed and pick up your room each morning," were the least of the instructions that came my way. I thought then and still do that growing up with my father was kind of like going to Marine Corps boot camp at Parris Island. The fact that he had was continually brought to our attention by the "Old Corps" memorablia that decorated his den. We all missed him—terribly. My mother kept the den exactly as it was the day he died. Looking in at the door one expected to see him sitting at his desk, at work on some deed or survey map that had to be in the mail the next morning.

Still, life must go on and my mother had quickly adapted; in fact, she almost blossomed. I wondered what she had gotten herself into lately and looked forward to hearing about whatever it was. While she didn't seek out trouble or turmoil, she had a knack for ending up in the middle of earth-shaking events that took place somewhere else. Like the bank robberies, for instance.

Big-time crime wasn't a regular thing in Mountain Water or Plainview. Neither was small-time crime during my school years. Oh, sure, being the '60s, we had the drug problems usual to the times and drunk-driving arrests (almost always the same individuals over and over again in each case), and a shoplifting or two, but never anything as exciting as a bank robbery. Actually, it hadn't been much before then when the bank opened up in Plainview. Prior to that one had to drive to the county seat under the mountain to conduct high finance. And low finance too, for that matter.

The first robbery happened about fifteen years ago. My brother and I had left the mountain top by then and were off making the world better for all mankind. It was mid-afternoon, just about the usual bank closing time of three o'clock. A few minutes before, the siren down on the firehouse had blown long, loud, and clear summoning all volunteers left in town—most had jobs or businesses elsewhere. A telephone call had come in reporting a two-car accident on the hairpin turn halfway down the mountain. Both cars were on fire and people were trapped inside them, the caller said. The fire truck and rescue squad van raced out of town, lights flashing, sirens blasting, and tires screeching. They were followed by the cars and pickups of the ever-present curious folks and those volunteers who had missed a ride on the official vehicles. Even the state trooper left his just-served coffee and pastry behind in Warm's Restaurant and took off in hot pursuit to take charge of the whole incident and be up front when the photographers arrived.

About forty-five minutes later, they were all back with puzzled expressions on their faces. They had found no wrecked cars, no fire, and no injured victims. The hairpin turn was clear when they arrived at the scene with traffic moving freely in both directions. A search up and down the mountain road disclosed everything to be normal.

However, in that forty-five minute interval, something else had happened in the empty town they had left behind. As the rescuers departed down one end of Main Street, a lone bank robber came up the other end. Or from some place; no eyewitness could later be located to place him as coming from any direction. In fact, no witness to anything outside the bank could be found, period. Everyone in town, it seemed, had headed down the mountain to witness the catastrophe taking place there—or supposed to be taking place there, that is. The only local witnesses to anything were the two tellers and the bank manager (it was a small bank).

Ethel Cummings, the head teller, said this tall, slim man wearing a ski mask walked in the door. She didn't think the ski mask was anything out of the ordinary, what with the ski center being just a few miles down the road. That is, she didn't think it was out of the ordinary until the investigator from the sheriff's office, who was taking her statement, reminded Ethel the ski center wasn't open in August, which is what it was then.

Whatever, this tall, slim man, wearing a ski mask, came up to Ethel's window and handed her a note and a canvas bag. The tall, slim man didn't say anything. He just stood there, Ethel said. The note was short; it said to keep quiet, put all the money within reach in the bag along with the note, lay flat on the floor, and don't raise any alarm for at least ten minutes. Well, Ethel did just what the note ordered. Sandy Burger, a cute local gal who had started work at the bank only a month before, wasn't sure just what was going on and pitched in to help Ethel fill the bag. All that took less than five minutes and the tall, slim man left the way he came (whichever way that was), carrying the bag full of cash (about $10 thousand, so later reports said) and the note. Justin Forbes, the bank manager, didn't know anything had happened until he came out of his office and saw Ethel and Sandy lying on the floor. Once he had the story from them, he rang all the alarms and telephoned for help, but no one came—all officialdom and most everyone else was out of town handling the tragic accident down on the hairpin turn.

When help did come and the police had all the facts, it was too late to give chase. They didn't know which direction to chase anyway. Ethel and Sandy could give no help in identifying the tall, slim man. "He was wearing a ski mask, you know," Ethel protested. This was before security cameras became a commonplace item in small banks, so the police had no film of the event. Too bad, some said, they would have loved to see movies of Ethel and Sandy cleaning out cash drawers and stuffing that canvas bag.

Where did my mother come in, you ask? Simple, she got caught in a road block. With nothing else to do, the state police, assisted by deputies from the sheriff's office and local law-enforcement people, set up road blacks at every road intersection within a ten-mile radius centered around the bank. Our big, rambling farmhouse wasn't within this circle and my father was at work. He and my mother had been invited to supper at the home of friends in Plainview. Since this would be on my father's route home, he planned on stopping there. My mother was to spend the afternoon with her friend, but not then being a driver, the friend's daughter drove down to pick her up.

The road blocks weren't in place when Carol made the drive to our house, but they were on the return trip. Of course, they were stopped although why cars were being checked heading toward the crime scene wasn't easily answered and neither could my father understand why two small women in a beat-up Volkswagon were stopped in the first place. After all, neither of the two were tall nor was either one wearing a ski mask. They were both slim, however so that must have been it, my father reasoned after he heard who it was who had stopped them.

"Where are you girls coming from?" asked the official force.

Turns out it was Andy Shiller, a constable with the Plainview squad. That explains everything, my father said when my mother told him who it was to which my mother replied, "Well, he was nice; he called me a girl."

The response to Andy's question should have been simple. It wasn't. Carol said she was coming from Plainview which, of course, was true—to an extent, anyway. My mother, ever ready to keep things straight said, "No, Carol, that's not right. Officer, we're coming from Mountain Water," which was also true that being where our farmhouse was.

Before Andy could sort that out, Carol protested. "No, I came from Plainview."

Now, Andy knew he was onto something. He wasn't sure just what, but he definitely needed some back-up. "You ladies better step out and lean up against the side of your car here. Give me your names and I'll check out a few things," he commanded. It was getting serious. In just a couple of minutes, they had gone from being girls, to being ladies.

Well, it was soon settled. Andy's radio for help to the command center that had been set up in the firehouse prompted a telephone call to Carol's mother. She explained just who the two were and how they happened to be on the road. Andy was ordered to let them continue on their way, which they did, but not before my mother let him know what she thought about the whole incident. "Do you know, I could have ended up in jail," she told my father that evening.

"I really doubt it," he replied. "Andy probably doesn't know where the jail is."

For all that, the robber was never caught. "The investigation is still open," was the continuing report. Probably it still is, although most of the locals have pretty much forgotten the whole thing. All except my mother, that is.

The second robbery wasn't at the same bank; however, it was in a village about the same size as Plainview. Great Valley was two or three towns and another county to the west and nestled on the near shore of one of the many Catskill Mountain reservoirs that supplied clear, pure water to the residents---pure and unpure alike---of New York City. It had a stop light at the intersection of two state highways, which put it on a higher level than Plainview. Not the stop light, but the fact that two numbered highway routes crossed in the center of town. Plainview had a stop light, but only one major highway. Of course, Great Valley National(?) Bank took up one corner of the intersection.

It was about five years later and well along in the afternoon (far along, if one considered banker's hours, that is) on a Tuesday in June. The bank was empty, except for three tellers up front and two managers hunched over their desks in the back adding up numbers or whatever it is that bank managers do. Even though the earlier robbery had occurred only twenty miles away, this and other mountain-top banks hadn't considered it necessary to employ bank guards. They had, however, installed security cameras or, more specifically, camera. None of the banks, including the ones in Plainview and Great Valley, had more than one camera. The one at Great Valley wasn't focussed at or toward the door; instead, it was off to one side and looked down on the line of teller's windows. All one had to do to avoid having his or her face photographed was to look the other way. The local teen-aged boys thought it great sport to peer directly into the lens and make weird faces for posterity.

Well familiar with the location of the camera, the bank patron (he was that as he came in the door whatever happened next) sidled up to the camera and draped a blanket over the lens. It was only seven feet or so off the floor, so that wasn't too difficult a feat. That odd behaviour and the fact the patron wore a ski mask (in June?) alerted the tellers this wasn't to be an ordinary deposit or, more likely, withdrawal. The note and canvas bag handed over the counter by the silent, tall, slim person confirmed this. "Fill it up," the note said or words to that effect the best the receiving teller, June Berry, could recall. The note was no longer available to confirm the exact wording. As had been the case five years earlier, the note was stuffed in the canvas bag along with the cash which, so later reports said, amounted to nearly $20 thousand. Obviously, pickings in Great Valley were better than Plainview had yielded.

The whole transaction (if one could call it that) took only a few minutes. Since bank closing had been imminent, no other customers were in the bank and, thus, witnesses to the event consisted of only the three tellers. The sidewalks outside—on all four corners of the intersection—were also empty at that time of day. Well, they were most of the time, not just at three o'clock. Shoppers in the drug store across the way told police they had seen a tall, slim person come out of the bank about then. Yes, he was carrying a sack of some kind. No, he didn't seem to be in a hurry.

One of the shoppers thought this person got into a green car that had been parked just down the street headed east. Or, maybe it was north. Sally Judd, that's who it was, said she never could keep directions straight, but the car did seem to be going to Greene County, so it must have been east. The other two shoppers wore trifocals and couldn't see that far. They didn't know what color the car was or even if a car had been parked there in the first place. If Sally said it was green, it must have been green. They had known her since she was a little girl (They were well along in years. Not Sally; the two other shoppers.) and had never known her to lie about anything.

Obviously, the assorted police who responded to the alarm raised by the bank manager didn't have much to go on. They did have a green car (or thought they had a green car) heading east on Route 23 into the next county. That put the sheriff at a disadvantage; his jurisdiction extended only to the county line. The state police, who showed up in force were under no such constraint and fanned out in all directions, set up road blocks, and put out all-points bulletins (or whatever they're called) describing the tall, slim man (that's about all the description they had) driving a green car. However, that's all the information Uncle Harry and Aunt Sarah needed.

Uncle Harry was my father's brother. He was a quiet man and pretty much had to be. Aunt Sarah did most of the talking, seeming always to have something to say and prone to use off-color words to make her point. Uncle Harry was some kind of chief in the Mountain Water volunteer fire company and had a scanner so he could get early alerts on fire emergencies. I think it was Aunt Sarah who got the most use out of the thing. It was always on and set at high volume. Whenever we were visiting at their home, every conversation was punctuated with calls and messages of all kinds filling in the background. I don't remember any of these having to do with the fire company; at least, I can't recall Uncle Harry ever bolting out the door on any emergency. However, they did keep up on the official doings of the other fire departments and police units all over the county. Of course, they heard the bulletin about the green car heading in their direction.

About this time, my mother was out on the porch washing windows. A car she didn't recognize pulled in the driveway and onto the old farm road that ran behind the barn, across the field, and into the woods. My father was at work and not near a telephone. Since she knew Uncle Harry had taken the day off from work and lived only a couple of miles away, she thought to call him to come and investigate the strange car. She didn't get Uncle Harry, she got Aunt Sarah, which was no surprise. Uncle Harry never answered the telephone; Aunt Sarah always got there first and then relayed the conversation to him. This one went something like this.

"Is Harry there?" my mother asked.

"Yes. Did you hear about that goddamned robbery over in Great Valley?"

Of course, my mother hadn't, but decided not to ask knowing she would have to listen to a complete run-down of something she no interest in—or thought she didn't anyway. "Tell Harry a car just drove through the field and into the woods and I wish he'd go see who it is. We didn't give permission to anyone to go out there."

Aunt Sarah passed that information on to Uncle Harry, who sat glued to the messages on the scanner. "Ask her what color the car is."

"Harry wants to know what color the car is."

"I think it was green," my mother replied.

"Holy shit, Harry, it's green," Aunt Sarah exploded and hung up the telephone.

My mother thought that about as strange as the car. Aunt Sarah never ended any conversation that abruptly. Then she thought it was because both of them were coming to her aid as quickly as possible. When they didn't show up in the next few minutes, she went back out on the porch to continue the window washing and to watch for them and the green car. She didn't get very far along in her work when she heard a voice.

"Go back in the house, lady, and stay there."

Startled, she looked in the direction of the command and saw a state trooper standing, with drawn pistol, behind the big spruce tree in the center of the lawn. Then she noticed three police cars pulled to the side of the road in front of the house and a fourth blocking the driveway. A number of troopers—all with pistols at the ready—were heading for the barn and points beyond. The trooper behind the spruce tree came onto the porch, took my mother by the shoulders and hurried her into the living room. A couple of plainclothes men arrived shortly and began questioning her about the car. "What make was it? How many people were in it? How fast was it going? Was it a coupe or a four-door?" It was pretty bewildering.

After all that, it turned out to be quite benign. The man in the green car (Yes, it was, indeed, green.) had been cutting wood on the farm out back about a year before, had left some tools in the woods, and had come back for them. He didn't think anyone would mind if he used the road just that once, but probably should have stopped at the house to ask and now wished he had. If my mother had been overwhelmed by the multitude of policemen swarming all over the place, imagine how the wood cutter must have felt when he realized he was surrounded by a bevy of uniformed lawmen with each officer holding a gun pointed directly at his chest.

The real green car wasn't found that day and neither was the tall, slim man in the ski mask nor the canvas bag with its $20 thousand. A couple of years later, some deer hunters did find the car parked behind an abandoned house at the end of a dead-end road up on the ridge only about a mile from our house. It had been there for some time by the looks of things, but yielded no clues to help in identifying the driver who had left it there. The owner was tracked down and, as it turned out, the car had been stolen two years before from the municipal parking lot down at the county seat while he was there on business. He had reported the theft at the time, he said, and his story checked out with the police records of the incident.

Although the trail was cold, the police searched in and around the abandoned house. They found nothing, but when they walked up the old, long-unused road that ran from the dead end at the house over the mountain and down into the next valley—next county, actually—they did see what they thought might be the tracks of a motorcycle. They couldn't be sure, of course, the weather and time over the two intervening years had erased any clear tracks. It was in a couple of dry, sheltered spots where they picked up the tire tracks or, at least, what looked like tire tracks. They questioned folks along the road down the other side of the mountain, but came up with nothing. Time had obscured memories as well as tire tracks.

So, that investigation is also continuing but, quite frankly, not too enthusiastically. The trails are old as well as cold; one fifteen years ago and the other, ten. Chances were remote the robber would ever be caught. That much had been decided; both robberies had been committed by the same person. The official force, Andy Shiller included, had reached that conclusion and there the matter rested.

It would be fun to spend a few days with my mother and I looked forward to it. She hadn't gotten herself involved in any other crime sprees, but I knew her life was full of other odd, funny, and interesting events. And, holy shit, it would be good to see Uncle Harry and Aunt Sarah again.

FOUR

THE TRAVEL AGENT called to remind me I still hadn't made up my mind about renting a car. Actually, I had and the decision yet to be made should have been simple. Which one? My options were an economy car, which included a charge for mileage, or a luxury car, which involved a flat fee with no mileage. I had already agonized over the rental for about a week when the agent called. Like most things in my life, I probably took it a little too seriously. The luxury car was more realistic because it turned out to be the cheaper of the two, considering Plainview was nearly a two-hour drive from the airport. Also, I would probably be here and there during the two weeks, and it certainly would be more comfortable. And, who wouldn't want to show up at their class reunion in a Lincoln Town Car? On the other hand, what would that and they say about me?

"Mom, what's the big deal? It's just a car." Emma sounded a little aggravated and acted it as she pulled out barely missing the rear fender of the late model Mercedes parked in front of us.

Her learner's permit was only four days old and I was letting her drive home from school while I sat in the copilot's seat trying not to hold onto the door handle, but did anyway. Actually, I was scared to death, which didn't make much sense when I remembered my own first few times behind the wheel.

My grandmother had been my driving instructor. I was kind of glad when she volunteered for the job. "You don't want your father to teach you. You'll never do anything to suit him. Then, you'll get upset and run into a tree or, even worse, somebody's mail box. Besides that, he isn't as good a driver as he thinks he is. I'll teach you how to drive."

It was quite an adventure; my grandmother was a legend behind the wheel. The mail was never late when she and my grandfather had the contracts for the two star routes that left from the Mountain Water post office. In fact, the mail on her route was usually early. She didn't let me drive up the valley, but after we had passed the last mail box, she pulled over and I drove the ten miles back to the post office. She was never concerned about my errors, telling me, "Just keep calm, it'll all work out." As I look back on it, I realize she seemed more interested in reading the post cards we had collected on the route. The result was I drove just like she did—too fast and with purpose. "Good night, El! Slow down," was pretty much of a litany recited by Roger every time we traveled together and I was in the driver's seat. Now, here I was holding on with both hands and pulling the seat belt strap up a notch.

Just a car, indeed. My hippie sensibilities were at odds with my middle-class desires. "Oh Em," I said, feeling sheepish and over-whelmed. Idiotic, is more like it. "I don't want to go up there looking like little Miss Middle Class. I mean, what about selling out to the establishment? What about the military industrial complex? I don't want them to think I've gone over to the other side."

"Mom, you have gone over to the other side. It's no big deal. You're the only one who still cares."

She was right. I was the only one who still cared. I realized that the day I saw Eric Clapton in a beer commercial. How was it possible that a generation bent on forsaking the materialistic goals of our parents and vowing to spend our lives meditating in a commune brought us the tanning bed and personal computers? No wonder Abbie Hoffman committed suicide.

"Mom, I know you're being real serious about this." Emma put her hand on mine in a gesture of sympathy. I appreciated her thoughtfulness, but would have preferred she keep both hands on the steering wheel. "It's not a crime to enjoy nice things. Life isn't as black and white as you try to make it out to be. It's possible to drive around in a big car and still be a decent human being."

She changed lanes without looking in her mirrors. I tried not to gasp, but did anyway. "Sorry," she grinned at me. "Look, we're in a nice car right now and we're not thinking of starting a war."

Well, no, although I did wonder if we might not end up in an emergency room before the day was over. I was beginning to think those parents who hire an uninvolved, totally objective professional to teach their children to drive had the right idea. It was either that or I was going to have to start ordering Valium by the case, then, I remembered my grandmother, unconcerned, stoic, busily reading post cards as we sped down the valley road and realized her advice, "Keep calm, it'll all work out," still applied.

"Mother, get a nice car. Have a fun time. This is a big event for you. I know how you loved school and you'll love the reunion. All your real friends will be there. You're always saying those people up there are the only ones in the whole wide world who really know you."

She drove in silence—for a few minutes. "Except for me and Dad, of course."

I wondered if she was waiting for me to clarify those things I had said so many times. "You know, don't you, you and your dad are the most important people in my life. The people I went to school with are close in a different way. We knew each other from the first days in kindergarten until we were graduated. They know me in a special way, where I came from. We were together so long, we nearly forgot we came from different backgrounds and that some had advantages while others did not."

"So, what's the problem? If you were all that close, a Lincoln Town Car isn't going to change their opinion of you." She grinned, "What color are you going to ask for?"

"The car? I don't know. Black, maybe. I suppose they'll think I'm married to ...."

"A mobster." She grinned again. "Well, we won't tell."

"Maybe I'll ask for red," I said, as we finally pulled into the driveway, all in one piece. By then, I had forgotten how scared I had been at the start. It had worked out, after all.

I should have expected the subject would come up eventually, but I was taken by surprise when Emma asked, "Will all of your old boy friends be there?"

Oh, jeez, I thought, I hope not. "I didn't exactly have a cast of thousands when it came to boy friends. I had a few, one or two. I expect they'll be there. With their wives, I'm sure."

"Why isn't Daddy going with you?"

Another good question. The answer was I had gone to his ten-year class reunion. On the way home, we vowed we would never go to another one together. I didn't know anyone he went to school with and his friends weren't interested in me anyway. I missed all the inside jokes, didn't understand the old stories, had no idea who they were talking about, and was miserably uncomfortable and bored, while Roger had the time of his life. Except when he was worrying about me being uncomfortable and bored.

I spent most of the evening being confronted by people who gazed at my name tag and said things like, "I don't remember you," or "Who were you before you got married?" I explained over and over the reason they didn't remember me was because I had gone to school in New York State. When I told them I was married to Roger, every single one responded, with a big grin, "Oh, you mean Pookie. Well, it's nice to meet you." This last was said as they backed away, looking hopefully for someone who would be a little more stimulating.

I waited until we were in the car ready to start for home. Even though this was in the days before the concept of designated drivers, I was at the wheel, since I had spent the entire evening nursing one scotch and water, which had turned out to be mostly water as drinks usually are at those kinds of parties. Before I turned the key in the ignition, I looked at Roger and said, "Pookie?" He just smiled and told me it was a long story. I'm still waiting for it to be told.

Clothes were the biggest problem. I wasn't sure if I should go to the "Get Reacquainted Cocktail Party" in a cocktail dress and if I should take jeans or shorts or both for the Sunday picnic. And what about the reunion itself? Emma, who believed every occasion, no matter how insignificant, provided a good reason to visit the Express down at the mall, thought maybe we should do a little shopping. "Forget it," I told her. "They haven't seen me in a quarter of a century. They don't know what kind of clothes I wear today. They probably won't recognize me no matter what I'm wearing. I'll just take a few things and decide when I get there."

I packed my suitcase ten times. Suitcases actually. After all, I was going to be away for two weeks. I eventually ended up with all the things I had packed on the first try. Plus an iron. Perplexed, Emma asked, "You don't think your friend has an iron?"

"I don't know. She probably does. On the other hand she's never been married and probably sends her laundry and cleaning out. Maybe she has a maid come in. She's a doctor, you know, and probably doesn't have time for such mundane things as ironing."

"Sometimes, Mom, you can be really weird." She started out the door. "Don't forget to have your roots touched up." At that point I almost decided not to go, but I did.

What would I find, I wondered. I expected the usual forty-something collection of Volvo drivers, Rolex wearers, and super-achievers, along with a smattering of vegetarians, New Agers, born-again Christians, and twelve steppers; that is, the usual bunch who showed up at every wine and cheese party whether invited or not. Housewives on Xanax and Evian, who routinely reached their children's beeper numbers via cellular phone. High-powered men with pony tails flirting with women wearing power suits and haircuts. Divorced people by the dozen, who spent their holidays at the airport, greeting children arriving on the incoming flight with visions of guilt-induced gifts from the Gap, while the current spouse ushered stepchildren to the boarding gate in another part of the terminal. And, then, there would be ones like me, still wondering what the hell they were going to do when they grew up.

I expected my classmates not to recognize me as a super-achiever, but as a non-achiever, basically, who began in a fury of drama all those years ago, only to wake up twenty-five years later to discover my finest accomplishment had been to relocate from a small town in the Catskill Mountains to a small town at the foot of Kennesaw Mountain in Georgia. Talk about high excitement.

The reunion seemed to begin in the Albany airport, that miniscule bastion of arrivals and departures which had so fascinated me the first time I entered it in the early 60s. I remember being absolutely taken with the costumes (not uniforms) worn by the Braniff stewardesses in those days: pillbox hat, spike heels, straight skirt. This was the last word in high fashion to a hick raised "on the mountain." We always referred to anything down in the Hudson Valley as "under the mountain" as in, "We were under the mountain yesterday. Bought a dress at Jamesway and had a grilled cheese for lunch at Newberry's."

"Bought a dress at Jamesway!" Emma would squeal, if she knew what a Jamesway was. Emma dressed impeccably according to the rules of *Seventeen* and *Sassy* and wouldn't deign to purchase even her underwear at Jamesway. I wondered if it was still there; I could use a new garden hose.

As I waited at the car rental counter, I saw three of my classmates, the ones I had been thinking of as the Carolina contingent since reading the directory that came with the announcement of the reunion. Two were from South Carolina and one from North Carolina along with what I assumed to be a collection of husbands and unusually small children in tow. Great looking husbands. Whatever else they did, these guys obviously ran and lifted weights. The age of the children, as well as the presence of husbands, made me think all were second marriages.

We didn't fall on one another immediately, although I remembered the first time I saw these women. We were four-year-olds, approaching kindergarten orientation with much trepidation. Our moms sat on little wooden chairs while Mrs. Van Loan tried to loosen us up with a turn on the wooden floor as she banged out something lively on the piano. "Let's all dance like butterflies, children!" she encouraged, as we timidly took center stage. The only one, as I remembered it, who seemed to exhibit any freedom of movement was still looking pretty much like a free spirit, wearing a tied-dyed

skirt and loose shirt, sandals, pushing a rubber-tired stroller containing a child of, maybe, eighteen months, wearing one of those head-
bands with a flower on it. My theory is these things must be glued
to the heads of toddlers. I couldn't even keep a hat on Emma. We
one-time classmates smiled at each other, tentatively. We were sure
we knew one another, but I bet myself she was thinking the same as
I, which was this can't possibly be Debbie Borden, because she looks
so old.

Finally, since I was alone and at the end of the line, I made the
first move. "You're Debbie, aren't you?"

"Ellyn?" She looked me straight in the eye, probably counting
my crow's feet. "I thought it was you. You look wonderful."

I should have looked wonderful. I had spent weeks at the tanning
beds, had my roots done yesterday, my nails the day before that, as
well as a massage and facial. Even my luggage was new. I did look
wonderful, compared to what I usually looked like, but I still looked
my age, which must have been a shock. "Well, I don't know about
wonderful. But this looks wonderful. Is this yours?" I pointed to the
stroller occupant, wondering why I referred to this charming child
as a this, since the headband announced she was a girl. That was the
whole point of the headband, I decided.

Debbie got that look, the same as I did during Emma's toddler-
hood. I now regreted putting people through it. "Yes, this is Borden."
Aha, she had fallen prey to the Southern habit of naming a daughter
with the mother's maiden name. "She's almost two." Pretty calm
two, I thought, to be sitting so placidly in a stroller with people
talking and milling all about her.

"She's lovely," I said, and she was, although I now realized she
was a classic Down's syndrome baby. I had seen a number of these
children lately, as women my age heeded the siren call of their
biological clocks. "Didn't you, don't you, have older children?"

"Oh, yes, Starla is fourteen." This was the kind of name we gave
our children in the early 70s, when we didn't know any better. "She
lives with her dad. Most of the time." She sighed, the universal sigh
of mothers of teenagers. There ought to be a support group, and
probably was. It was a tough existence, it really was, and must be

made almost impossible by divorce. I had seen the manipulation that happens when normal teenage angst takes the form of moving to dad's and, then, back to mom's. Thank God, Roger and I had stayed married if only to avoid all that.

Debbie took me by the arm and pulled me toward a beautiful woman in a peach-colored, silk blouse and shorts, leather loafers, and anklets. "You remember Jane, of course." God, what boring names our parents gave us. No Starshines or Moonbeams in this crowd. Jane was radiant, holding hands with a tall, composed, gray-haired man. Jane and I had been close friends, spending the night with each other, calling boys all night long and hanging up on them when they answered the phone. I regretted that we hadn't seen each other recently. We lived, at most, only three or four hours apart. I found that funny and so did Jane, apparently, as she smiled and said, "Now, isn't this logical, coming all the way to Albany to see each other. I've thought of trying to locate you, but I never quite got around to it."

"You look fabulous, Jane," I said, and she did. She had some kind of glow.

She laughed and waved her hand, "You should have seen me last year when I had no hair." She smiled at her husband, who smiled back, tenderly. Cancer. That explained the radiance and her husband's protective presence. Death which had been held at bay, but could return at any moment, tended to add another dimension to life. We put our arms around each other. I was truly glad to see her. "You remember Jay?" I did. I remembered the wedding, the golden couple at the altar. I even remembered the wedding dress, a confection of satin and lace. I looked over her shoulder at Debbie and at Mary, who was standing in the background, waiting for her chance at reintroduction. God, I thought, I was going to be doing this all weekend.

I held out my hand to Mary, who squeezed it. "You do look wonderful, Ellyn," she said. "I'm so happy to see you." She was subdued and quickly retreated to her place at the side of her husband, who was a looming, disconcerting presence. "You look good too, Mary," I said, although I didn't mean it. She had the defeated demeanor of an abused wife.

We all stepped back, to get a better look at each other. The aging process had ceased to amaze us and we were looking at friends, people who knew us, people we cared about. Life hadn't been easy for these, my friends. My concerns about myself began to sound like whining, which it was. I was sad for them, but I was happy, too. There would never again be people in my life with whom I felt so comfortable.

The car rental staff had suddenly begun a flurry of activity and presented us with forms to sign, while asking for our credit cards. Please, God, I prayed, don't let them refuse my card. This was a strong possibility and one I had been worrying about. But they handed it back without incident, which made me think Roger must have payed a little extra on the bill. I showed my insurance card and received the keys to a Buick Park Avenue. "Maroon," said the car rental clone person. "It's in space 625." Good Lord, I thought, they have 625 cars to rent at the Albany airport—what a difference a quarter of a century makes.

FIVE

HE ROUTE out of the terminal complex was as confusing at Albany as at any other airport of comparable size. The road wound about in a series of curves, ellipses, and spirals until I was sure I was going to end up back at the car rental place and space 625. The fact that the only times I had been at this airport was years ago and my father was then doing the driving didn't help much. However, by paying attention to the numerous signs, arrows, and painted lines and words on the pavement, I found my way to the Northway. The points of the compass have always been a mystery to me much to the consternation of my father, a land surveyor who could find his way out of the deepest woods in the middle of the night just by looking at the stars and observing the way the moon cast shadows of the trees—or so he said. I correctly decided I should take the south-bound lanes because the signs said the Thruway was in that direction and I knew that was the next route I had to watch for.

Fortunately, it was the middle of the afternoon and I didn't have to contend with hordes of state workers rushing for home. The road was clogged, however, with shoppers heading to and from the Wolf Road malls to pick up after-Memorial Day bargains. I made the Thruway toll barriers without incident and accepted the ticket thrust at me by a faceless body occupying the booth in the green-lighted lane I lined up with. Touching the accelerator lightly, the car bolted forward with a screech of tires I wasn't prepared for. As I left the entrance ramp and blended into the swift-moving traffic, I flicked on the automatic pilot. What a great car, I thought, my grandmother would have loved it. Well, maybe not, she was more of a four-on-the-floor person who liked to drive instead of being driven by a vehicle crammed full of electronic gadgets that anticipated every whim of the person at the wheel.

Soon after the Thruway turned southerly at Interchange 23 (I knew it was south because a sign as big as the side of a barn said so), the Catskill Mountains hove into view over the horizon. The Black-head Range reared up from the plains like a trio of giants. All of these mountains----Blackhead, Black Dome, Thomas Cole running left to right (I said that because I'm not sure if they run east to west or west to east)----reach nearly to 4,000 feet. In fact, early records put Black Dome at 4,004 feet to make it one of only three Catskill mountains extending over that magical figure. Of course, 4,000 feet isn't much when compared to the elevations of the great ranges of the world, but to a native Catskiller (or Catskillian, I'm never sure of that either), who spent nearly half her life in Georgia, it's right up there. I looked again at the three hulks and named them once more. My father had drilled the names of most of the mountains of the Catskills into my brother's head and mine time after time until he was sure we had them in the right place with the right name. "You should know their names," he said, "They have personalities, too, and are a part of our heritage."

I left the Thruway at the Catskill exit and took the well-remem-bered turns to Route 23A. Yes, the Jamesway was still there, but looked much smaller than I had recalled. I didn't stop, the garden hose could wait. The highway rose gradually as it neared Palenville and, then, climbed steeply as soon as it crossed the Kaaterskill. The Buick took it in stride, not even flinching as the Clove gapped precipitously on the right. The road twisted and turned as it steadily gained height and nearly came back on itself coming around the hairpin turn under Bastion Falls. Above Lookout Point, the Clove fell steeply on the left. Near the top at Haines Falls, I looked westerly (yes, I did know what direction it was) into a tumble of mountains and valleys all painted with the green of spring. "The land of the magnificent distance," my father had called these old hills quoting, he said, notes left by some old-time surveyor. This was home country.

As I drove down Main Street (here part of Route 23A), I looked for familiar places, but didn't find too many. A large sign, painted in psychedelic colors, announced "Tattoos by Wing." Yes, I agreed with Jan's description, it was a bit garish. Fortunately, it was counterbalanced by the staid and weathered sign in front of Warm's Restaurant.

Jan's office and home were in a big, white-painted, two-story house one block off Main Street on the other end of town. I purposely passed the turn and drove out of the village to the top of the hill where the road dropped toward the ski center. I pulled off here and parked. I stepped out in the warm sun and looked at the mountains extending, range after range, in front of me. I knew who they were; they seemed to nod back as I called them by name. It was hard to ignore Hunter, dead ahead and topped by the fire tower. It was a true 4,000-foot peak, the second highest in the Catskills. I drank in the fresh air and watched the sun paint shadows of the clouds across the ridges and valleys. Sometimes, one can go home again.

I turned the Buick around and went back up Main Street. The school stood majestically, kind of like a castle, on the hill. It looked the same; the brown-brick facade reflected the late afternoon sun. The building was nearly empty at this time of day. I saw a few teachers (my, how young they looked) scurry to their cars and a couple walking the long flights of concrete steps leading down to the sidewalk at the edge of the street. The school buses had left long ago. I turned in and slowly drove up the winding driveway and around the building. I didn't stop—Jan and and our classmates would visit for the open house on Saturday. I just wanted to experience the solidness of the place and a moment or two back in time. Careful with all this nostalgia, I cautioned, telling myself not to get too maudlin.

Jan was still holding office hours. She had told me to expect that. I parked in back of the house and went in through the kitchen. Her last words in our telephone conversation a week ago had been, "I'll leave the door open for you. Your room is down the hall on the left. Just move in and make yourself at home."

I did just that. The windows were open and a cool breeze blew through the house carrying the scent from the blossoms in the small flower bed under my window. Noticing the telephone on the night table, I dialed my mother's number to let her know I had arrived safe and sound. I let it ring ten times before deciding she must be on the road again. I then called home. Emma's first question was the important one, "What kind of car did you get and what color is it?"

Those notification obligations taken care of as good as they could be, I picked up a magazine from the coffee table in the living room and went out to the patio off the kitchen. I must have been more tired than I thought because I soon fell asleep in the well-padded lounging chair. I was jolted awake by a sound like a gun shot followed by the roar of a high-pitched engine being gunned into life. It settled down to a steady rumble and faded into the distance toward the center of town. As I leaned over to pick up the magazine that had slid from my lap onto the stone deck, the kitchen door slammed behind me.

"If that boy doesn't soon start taking care of himself he won't be around much longer."

Evidently office hours were over. Jan took the chair next to me. We exchanged no words of greeting even though we hadn't seen each other for years. It was that kind of friendship; when we did meet, it was as if we had been apart only since earlier in the day. We just picked up where we left off, no matter how long before that had been.

"Boy? What boy?" I asked, now fully awake.

"Oh, that Rory Hale, that's who," Jan replied with an obvious irration in her voice.

"He's not a boy anymore. Does he still have freckles?"

"Well, he may not be a boy, but he acts like one. Yes, he still has freckles. And tattoos all over the rest of his body. He doesn't eat right. He smokes too much and God knows what else he's doing to shorten his life span. He won't pay any attention to what I tell him. I don't know why he keeps coming in for regular appointments. And next time he roars in here on that damn motorcycle, I'm going out and take a scapel to the tires."

That pretty much covered it, I thought. "How are things otherwise?"

"Oh, all right. Sorry to run on, but I've been Rory's doctor for years and have watched his health run continually downhill. He has a bad heart and a lot of other problems, but doesn't seem to care. I don't know if I'm not getting through to him or what."

"That's too bad, but I suppose you have to expect an uncooperative patient now and then."

"That's just it," Jan replied. "I don't really consider him a patient. He's an old friend and I'm trying to help him. Well, enough of my problems—or problem, Rory seems to be the only one at the moment. I didn't think you'd want a big meal after your long trip, so I had Warm's bring up some sandwiches and salads and put them in the fridge this afternoon. And I've got a bottle of wine chilled."

I finally got my mother on the phone. She'd been helping out at the library that afternoon and had been there when I had called earlier. We hadn't yet decided when I would be coming to stay with her, but we now thought Tuesday would work out. By then, I would have all this reunion business behind me and be ready to focus on something else. Little did I know what the days ahead had in store.

Jan hadn't scheduled office hours for Friday, so we could have time to catch up on the local doings. Not that it would take long to do that. In our long telephone conversations, she had kept me current with the trials and tribulations of most everyone I remembered, especially those in our class who had remained in the area. All of them she had seen lately were planning on being at the cocktail party that evening and most would be at the actual reunion. We twenty-five-year veterans would be special at the reunion except, of course, for the half-century class. Do you suppose anybody was still left from the Class of '43, I wondered.

The reunion itself was for every class—young, old, and in-be-tween—along with teachers,—retired and otherwise (yes, a couple had been terminated)—custodians, bus drivers, cafeteria staff, and even members of the school board. Although he could have attended this annual event with his class or as a former school board person, my father never would go. "I don't care about seeing all those old people," he said each year when the notice arrived in the mail. Now that I was here, I was beginning to think maybe I didn't want to see them either. Of course, Jan and I didn't think we looked old, but what about the rest of the Class of '68.

Patty Sanderson had planned the cocktail party and Sunday picnic for our class. "Oh, you know Patty," Jan said. "She got everybody involved whether they wanted to be or not and assigned tasks just like we were part of her third-grade class. I had to hire the hall----actually the banquet room at the Cascade House----for the party and be sure bartenders were hired and well-stocked with liquid refreshment. Someone else, Janie, I think, got stuck with the food end of the deal. Now you know why your ticket cost so much."

We spent Friday driving and walking around town. We stopped in at Gary Grissom's law office across from the tattoo parlor with its garish sign. Gary's brass plate on the front of the building next to his office door came in a poor second, it seemed to me. Now that I had seen Wing's sign up close, I didn't think it was that bad. It certainly was an attention grabber. Gary wasn't in. "He's under the mountain. Down in Catskill for some political thing," Susie Carr told us. Susie had been treated well by the twenty-five years. She looked and dressed smart and seemed content with her place in life. I doubted she passed anyone into the inner sanctum of Gary's office either in person or by telephone if she didn't think they should be. On the other hand, I'm sure she never turned anyone away who really needed help whatever their place in life. I also imagined not too many of Gary's bills went unpaid for very long; Susie was obviously too efficient to let that happen.

The tattoo parlor was also an efficiently-run place as I found when we visited there; Jan taking me by the arm and literally propelling me across the street. She introduced me to Wing, the tattoo artist, who, it turned out was one of her patients as, I suppose, nearly everyone in town was seeing she was the only doctor around. Wing was a pleasant enough sort, a little rough around the edges and obviously able to hold her own in any circumstance that might arise. Leather seemed to be her fabric of choice, at least her wardrobe that day was heavy in that direction. The parlor was decorated with full-size examples of her work----on paper, I'm happy to say, not actual skin as had been used by the mistress of Belsen to fashion lamp shades. No, I assured her, I hadn't stopped in for a tattoo, only to say Hi to Rory, who happened to be out with her husband on a job. I didn't ask what the job was.

A few doors up from the tattoo parlor, we stopped at the Timmerman Hardware Store. It was now in the third generation of the same family ownership and probably would continue on into the fourth. It was unlikely any of the big chains, K-Mart, Walmart, or the like, would move onto the Mountain Top and crowd it out of business. Jamie wasn't there, his younger brother, who I always thought was an obnoxious kid, was in charge for the day, Jamie being off or some village business. "He is the mayor, you know," his brother informed us.

After that, we seemed to crisscross the street dodging traffic; it was, after all, a main route across the Catskills. First, we dropped in on Janie at her beauty shoppe—not shop, I'll have you know. Stanley was in at his real estate/insurance office and took time out to walk with us down to Warm's for a cup of coffee. While we were there Zeke pulled up at the taxi stand out front and came in to join us.

Seeing old friends—and they didn't look nearly as old as I thought they might—made the afternoon race along. We didn't, of course, run into everyone, but enough to make me glad I had decided to come after all. I looked forward to the party that evening when "We'll all be there" each of them told me. It was as if we were still young, still in school, and simply planning another get-together. Well, almost as if, that is.

SIX

THE CASCADE HOUSE was one of the oldest buildings in Plainview having started out as one of the early boarding houses on the mountain. Although it had soon been overshadowed by the grand hotels that perched on ledgey promontories to gaze down at the Hudson River, it survived. It had gone through a number of owners and deaths and rebirths over the years and somehow escaped being burned to the ground like so many other early wooden structures. Its name didn't fit its location; it was nowhere near a waterfall. In this respect, it was like so many other places and things that had been named by our forefathers apparently for the purpose of confounding later generations. Actually, it was on top of a hill on the edge of town above Washington Irving Lake. That, for some reason, did make sense. This part of the world was supposed to have been the site of Rip Van Winkle's long sleep, so it was appropriate to name some local site after the author of that tall tale.

Jan and I went early. She was under instructions from Patty to be one of the first to arrive to make sure everything was "in order." I just tagged along. Surprisingly, I changed my outfit only three times before deciding I looked dressed up or dressed down enough to fit in with the casual wear suggestion that had been included in the announcement. On the other hand, I might have tried another change or two had not Jan been standing by the back door tapping her foot and asking, "Aren't you ever going to be ready?"

We weren't the first. That was Patty, of course, although Janie, the food person, hadn't been too far behind. Patty, ever the overly-organized person, had set herself up just inside the door at a table covered with name tags laid out in alphabetical order and a pad on which she intended to list the name and exact minute of each arrival.

"Oh, my God," I thought, "Are we going to have to wear name tags?" Oh, yes, we were.

Patty greeted me with a hug and a passing kiss on the cheek before standing back. "How great to see you again, Ellyn. Here, let me pin on your name tag. It's been so many years and we probably will all look so different----mature, I mean----I thought we really would need name tags. I had my class paint a little flower on the corner of each one. Yours is a daisy, I think. Isn't it cute?"

What could I say? "Yes, it is nice," although I thought it looked more like a violet. I wondered if we were going to have to ask for permission to go the bathroom. I hoped those rooms would be designated with word signs saying "Men" and "Women" instead of those stupid stick figures that had become the rage a few years before. I never could decide which was which and more than once had ended up in the wrong one. Oh, well, if I got confused, I knew I could ask Patty to help me out of that dilemma----or any other I found myself in.

The room did look great; actually I had expected nothing else. A huge banner emblazoned with "CLASS OF '68" in big, red letters hung over the stage. Evidently this was the ballroom, I decided. Tables with chairs placed around them lined two sides of the room. Long tables, soon to be filled with all kinds of munchies and other snacky things most of us didn't need stood against the other wall along with two movable bars now being stocked by young men wearing white jackets. A four-piece band was setting up on the stage. My first thought was "I'll bet they'll open with the Alma Mater and I won't remember the words." No matter, I noticed a stack of papers on the corner of Patty's table and just knew what was printed on them.

It seemed as if everyone came at once. The schedule had said 7:00 P.M. sharp and no one dared incur Patty's wrath by being five minutes early or late. A line soon developed at the door as each waited to be signed in and handed their name tag. The band began to play. Slow stuff. They weren't too bad. The Alma Mater wasn't the first number, after all, but I was sure it was coming sometime during the evening.

I recognized many of my classmates, and they acted as if they knew who I was. I guess I hadn't gone completely over the hill after all. Those I didn't recognize were probably spouses and I was sure to be in for a long series of introductions. "Oh, El, I want you to meet my husband," or wife, as the case might be. I knew I wouldn't remember who was married to whom or what their names were. Maybe name tags weren't such a bad idea after all. The only trouble was the printing on them. It would have been all right twenty-five years ago, now it was too small for those of us who needed glasses but wouldn't wear them and those who had given in to bifocals. I spotted Gary Grissom right off. He was wearing his usual pinstriped suit, but I supposed that was casual wear to him.

Rory Hale was just the opposite. He had taken the casual wear advice to heart. From his motorcycle boots to his fringed leather jacket, he was about as casual as you could get. His red hair was thinning, but what could one expect when the law required bikers to wear helmets and shut out the sun from reaching it. His face was still flecked with freckles, but his eyes, which once had sparkled, seemed sad. He was alone; he hadn't married. I remembered Jan telling me years ago that his girl friend, a biker also, had been killed when a truck or a car or some other vehicle had overtaken her part way down the mountain and run into the back tire of her bike flipping it and her over the guardrail into the ravine far below. Those were the facts of the incident as reconstructed by the police anyway. The vehicle was never found, nor was anyone ever charged. Rory had never cared for any other girl, Jan had said.

"El, I'm so glad you came," Rory said as we met on the far side of the room. "I've always wondered where you were and if you were okay." He took my hand in both of his and held it. We didn't hug or go through any of the gushy stuff others used when greeting long-lost friends that evening. That kind of display of affection was foreign to each of us.

His eyes seemed to brighten for the moment and I was glad to see that.

"Let's sit here at one of these tables so we can talk," I suggested. He nodded his head in assent, but seemed reluctant to let loose of my hand. He squeezed it harder as we sat down.

"I had things I wanted to tell you. Things I couldn't tell anyone else. If only you'd been here. If you still lived here, I would have come to see you."

I didn't know what to say. In fact, I felt a little guilty. Rory and I had been friends in school, good friends, actually, special friends. We knew we could confide our private thoughts and dreams to each other and they would remain private, just between the two of us. We had long conversations back then. We had been important to one another and I should have remembered that.

"I wish I had been here. If I had known, we could have met somewhere in between."

"No, that wouldn't have been fair to you. It was my problem."

"Well, I'm here now and we can talk as long as you want. I remember how we used to visit about secret things. At least, they seemed so then."

Rory looked down at the table. "No, I can't, not tonight, maybe at the picnic on Sunday."

"Sure," I said. "We'll do that. I'm going to get a drink at the bar. Do you want me to bring you one?"

"Yeah. Whatever you have, I'll have the same. And ask Janie if she can fill up this bowl with whatever those nuts were."

Each of the tables had been provisioned with three large bowls filled by Janie when she had organized things earlier. One held popcorn (just the thing for people whose teeth were starting to disintegrate), another held an assortment of nuts, and the last was some chocolate-covered concoction that turned out to be roasted coffee beans. I had tried a couple, but didn't care for the sharp taste. Besides that, chocolate and coffee wasn't a very palatable mix as far as I was concerned. Once I decided what they were, I pushed the bowl away; even the smell of coffee after five was enough to keep me awake till the next morning. However, they hit the spot with Rory. He had emptied the bowl and was asking for more.

I wandered through the crowd, now getting louder as the initial hesitation at being together after so many years wore off. Perhaps the alcoholic beverages had helped that along; in fact, the biggest group seemed to be around the bars and I paused trying to find a way through. It took some time as each old friend had to reminisce about some foolish thing he or she and I had done back then. "Do you remember the look on Mr. Nelson's face when he opened his desk drawer and found that frog?" "Do you remember when Zack and Lucy ran off to Maryland and got married in the middle of the year? I was just shocked." "Do you remember when Billy hit that baseball through the cafeteria window when we were eating lunch?" "Do you remember when...?" Yes, I did remember. It seemed so long ago, but as I thought about it and looked around, the years melted away and it was almost yesterday.

It was too late in the day for a martini, so I ordered a vodka and 7Up. Two, actually, remembering Rory's request. I looked around for Janie, but couldn't locate her. It didn't matter, when I returned to the table, I saw that Rory had taken a bowl of the chocolate-covered whatevers from another one nearby.

I tried to draw him back to the subject of whatever it was that bothered him, but got the same response. "No, can't talk about that here. Wait till Sunday. We'll take a hike up to the site of the old Mountain House. It'll be quieter there."

We visited about a lot of things. He wanted to know what I did and about my family. I didn't ask about his troubles, but he told me anyway. "When I came back from jail, most people here wouldn't have anything to do with me. They didn't care much for Mack and Wing. We were the lower class, I guess. Then, when Lorna came along, she didn't fit in either. We were going to get married, you know. She was killed on her way down the mountain one day. It was an accident so they said, but I never quite believed that."

On and on he went. I listened as I had done all those years ago. It was an eerie thing, but all the while we talked, I had the sense we weren't alone. That someone else was listening too; that someone was watching us. I kept shifting around in my chair—looking over the crowd—but no one was acting out of the ordinary or seemed to be paying any attention to us. Still, the feeling persisted and it made me uneasy. Rory didn't appear to notice so I didn't mention it.

The subjects changed as passing friends sat with us for a few minutes before moving on. Jan appeared out of nowhere and Rory winced as she sat down. "Now I'm in for it. Here's the mother hen."

"How many drinks have you had, Rory? I told you yesterday your limit tonight was one."

"I remember. And that's all I've had. One drink when I got here; one drink El got for me; one Anna Buckley brought over. Why don't you talk to her? She's had more than I have," Rory laughed.

"She always has more than anyone else, but you're usually a close second. I'm not going to keep either one of you as patients if you don't straighten yourselves out. Soon it'll be too late and then I won't have to worry about it any longer."

We were interrupted by a fanfare blown by the trumpeter—well, he was more than that, each of the four band members were versatile, playing at least two instruments. No one had paid much attention to them before this. I hadn't noticed anyone on the dance floor. Not dancing, that is. A lot of people were on the dance floor as they crossed it on their way to the bar and back or as they stopped in the middle to talk to someone going the other way. They had our attention now or, rather, Patty did. She stood center stage tapping her fingernail on the microphone.

"Oh, great," Jan groaned. "I'll bet we're going to sing the Alma Mater."

Yes, we were. Patty finally got the crowd to silence. "It's been so long since we've sung this, I thought a few might have forgotten the words. I've had them printed and Janie and Susie are passing out the sheets. Now, all sing."

Well, we did and, funny thing, I noticed a tear or two in the eyes of some of most hardhearted in the crowd. I was a bit choked up myself. Patty then reminded us when we were supposed to arrive at the banquet the next evening and where the class tables would be located; not to forget the picnic at North Lake on Sunday; to remember to visit the school tomorrow. The doors would be opened at one o'clock so we could walk the halls, sit at the desks, and write our names on the blackboards. I suppose every class needs a social director and we sure had one of the best----Patty hadn't forgotten anything. As her list of reminders went on, I began to feel like a student in her third-grade room.

I realized Rory was no longer at our table and asked Jan, "Did you see where Rory went?"

"No, but I'm not surprised he left. He isn't much for all this social mixing stuff, especially after the way some of those here have treated him over the years. He's not going to the reunion tomorrow night. Too many people, he told me. He did say he was going to the picnic. That's more his kind of thing. If it gets too crowded, he can take a hike in the woods or go fishing down at the lake."

The evening wore on. A few couples did dance after a while. I made a trip to the food tables. Janie had managed a good variety of finger foods, dips, and munchie kind of stuff all sure to have more calories than necessary. I noticed some of my classmates had added an inch or two or three around the waist and more than a few pounds in places that could have done without any more padding.

All except Chris Rafferty, that is. He stood ramrod straight, tall, slim, ever the model of a person who lived and breathed law enforcement. Surprisingly, he wasn't wearing his uniform, but I did think he might have a shoulder holster under his loosefitting sports jacket. He rarely moved all evening from his stance at the end of one of the bars. I got the impression he was continually scanning the crowd looking for someone or something, although for who or what, I couldn't imagine. I had always looked up to Chris. Literally. He towered about a foot above me and was easy to spot in a crowd; his crew-cut head rose above those around him. I remembered going to a school dance with him in our sophomore year. I never saw any of the other couples on the floor; my nose was buried in Chris's chest and I couldn't see left or right.

As the old clock on the wall neared midnight, the crowd began to thin out. And why not? We were reaching the age when we dropped off in our chairs in the middle of a favorite television show or woke with a start when the book we had been reading slid from our lap and hit the floor with a bang. Besides that, we had two days of demanding social activity yet to go.

As I yawned for what must have been the tenth time, Jan suggested, "Why don't you go on home, I'll stay for a while to help wind things up—or down. I'll catch a ride with Patty or Janie. One of them can drop me off."

Not many were left by that time. Gary Grissom was still debating some legal point with whoever would listen. This time around, he had Dave Solomon backed against one of the bars. Seeing that Dave was anxious to find a way out, I walked over on the pretense of saying "Good Night" to each of them. Dave smiled (with gratefulness said the expression on his face). "Yes, it has been a good night and I should be getting on my way."

The mistake was mine. With one audience gone, Gary turned the conversation to me. "I've got to be going, too," I said hurriedly and edged toward the door.

Gary was, however, not one to give up easily and I suppose that's why he had gained the respect of others in his profession. "I'll walk along with you," he offered, and he did.

It was a starlit night and warm. Peepers or frogs or some kind of animals were putting up a holler down at the marshy end of the lake. Another sound—kind of like a groan—came from the depths of one of the lounge chairs scattered about the wide porch. Looking closer, we saw it was Rory. Both his eyes were closed and he seemed to having trouble breathing. "You stay here," I said to Gary, "I'll go get Jan."

That roused Rory from his stupor or whatever state it was he was in. "No. Don't get her. Just help me home. I didn't think I should try it myself on the bike and was waiting for you."

Did he think I was going to drive his motorcycle, I wondered? It was still there all right; I saw it parked in the corner of the lot off the end of the porch. "I don't even know where he lives," I said, questioning Gary. "What shall we do?"

"I walked over," he replied. "We can take him in your car. I'll ride along to show you where he lives. It's up a flight of stairs in back of the tattoo parlor. I can help him to his apartment."

That roused Rory again. "No, you don't have to go. I'll tell her where to go. I can make it up the stairs. You go on home."

With that, Rory heaved himself out of the chair and steadied himself by grabbing the porch railing. With Gary on one side and me on the other, we guided him down the steps and across the lot to the Buick. "Oh, no," I thought. "Don't let him be sick on that red fabric interior."

"Good luck," Gary said as he held the door for me on the driver's side. "I'll tell Mack or Wing in the morning where the motorcycle is."

It was only a few blocks to the tattoo parlor. They weren't really blocks. The roads were more a network of random streets following no pattern and had been carved across convenient breaks in the land by the founding fathers.

It took only a few minutes to get there. "Pull around back," Rory directed. I did and saw a flight of stairs leading to a second-story landing. "I live up there," he pointed.

I helped Rory out of the car. "I'll walk you to your door."

"No, you don't have to. I'm perfectly all right," he said just before he tripped on the bottom step and would have fallen had he not grabbed the railing with both hands. "Well, maybe a little less than all right," he laughed.

"I guess," and I laughed too. "I'll just follow behind to make sure you don't come all the way down before you get all the way up."

It took a few minutes, but we made it. "Give me your key and I'll open the door."

He searched in all his pockets and, after finally locating it, handed it to me. "Oh hell, it's not locked. I forgot to lock it. Doesn't matter, I haven't got anything anybody would want." Sure enough, the door popped open as he fell against it.

I flipped on the switch just inside. The light showed a large room lined with bookcases, the shelves filled with books and framed photographs. Many of these were of a pretty, blonde girl either astride a motorcycle or standing beside one. That must be Lorna, I guessed. The furniture and other furnishings were clean and neatly placed. It wasn't at all like I had expected.

Rory noticed my surprise through the haze that clouded his eyes. "I take care of the place by myself. I don't let many people in here. Thanks for helping me. I'll be okay now. I'll see you tomorrow maybe, but for sure on Sunday at the picnic. Don't forget we made a date to go on a hike."

Obviously, I was being dismissed and rightly so. I couldn't do much more now. Rory seemed to have regained some of his senses and equilibrium now that he was in familiar surroundings. "No, I haven't forgotten. We'll talk over old times then."

I left him standing there, gazing at the blonde girl's framed portrait that sat on the stand beside what was obviously his favorite chair. I set the snap lock and closed the door quietly as I went out. It was dark in the little parking space at the bottom of the stairs. The bright stars did little to light my way. The interior light relieved the darkness when I opened the car door but blinded me for a second. I got the impression of a person or the shadow of a person moving behind the corner of a shed on the other side of the open area. I looked again, but saw nothing. As I backed around, I maneuvered the car so the headlights shone on the building and the trees behind it. Nothing was there. It must have been a limb on one of the trees, I concluded. It was no wonder I was seeing things. The last hour had been a strange experience. I didn't know what had happened to Rory once he left our table. He had had a few drinks, but not enough to knock him out like that. Most of us had more than one drink, but were all right. Must be Rory's health was more precarious than I knew even though Jan had said he should be taking care of himself a lot better that he had been.

It was a short drive back to Jan's house. She wasn't there yet. I let myself in the back door with the key she had given me. It didn't take long to get ready for bed. I heard Jan come in just as I pulled the blanket up to my chin. It had been a busy and long two days. I was tired and fell asleep hoping Rory was sleeping easily too. If only I had known how deep his sleep was to be that night.

SEVEN

TO SAY I slept the sleep of the dead would be more than a little prophetic (pathetic, actually) considering what happened that night. I slept soundly, but was troubled by dreams. In one, a telephone rang. I kept hearing it, but couldn't find it; I ran from room to room in some sort of crazy house with no hallways or stairs, just rooms, but none of them had a telephone. When I got up the next morning, I learned a telephone call had come for Jan much earlier. In a later dream, I kept hearing another persistent ringing and ended up on a similar search in that same crazy house of many rooms. That had been Jan's doorbell, I found out later.

I felt someone gently shaking me by the shoulder and opened one eye. It was Jan. "Here's a cup of hot coffee. Drink that. When you have your wits about you, come on into the kitchen." She set the mug on the night stand and left the room, closing the door behind her.

My travel clock said 9:30, so it was time I was up and about, anyway. I sat on the edge of the bed and held the steaming mug in both hands. It was nectar almost. The sun streamed in over top of the drapes covering the window, and a light breeze blowing through the opening I had left at the bottom ruffled them back and forth. It was going to be a great day to visit the school. I heard a door close and voices and, then, the slam of car doors and the sound of a car as it left down the driveway. Must be an early-morning patient, I thought.

I pulled on my robe, stuck my feet in slippers, and scuffed down the hall to the kitchen. Jan sat at the table turning her coffee mug round and round and looked up expectantly. "You'd better sit down for this one. It isn't going to be fun."

I felt a tightening in my chest as if someone had squeezed my heart. I'm sure it skipped at least one beat and maybe more. "Oh?" was all I could muster, before sitting down as directed.

"I don't know if you heard any of the commotion that's been going on here for the last couple of hours. I went out for a while and some people have been here. You will be as sad and shocked as I. Rory was found dead this morning."

Shocked was a poor description of how I felt, poleaxed might be a better word. It didn't sink in; I couldn't believe Jan's words; I couldn't accept what she had said. I wanted to go back to bed and start the day over. "Dead? How can he be dead? He was all right when I left him. What happened? Dead? I don't want to believe it."

"I couldn't believe it either when Wing called for me to come. She had gone up about seven to see why he hadn't come down to leave for work with Mack. Whenever she had to get Rory under motion before, she said she just knocked on the door because he always kept it locked. However, when she knocked this time, it swung open. She found him, sitting in his chair. He didn't respond when she called, so she went in to wake him. When she touched him, she realized his skin was cold. She ran down to her place and called me."

"Oh, my. That's awful." I still couldn't assimilate what I was hearing as facts. I didn't want to. I wanted to reject it all.

"From the condition of his body, I would say he died soon after midnight, one o'clock or so. It's up to the coroner to determine that, but I'm sure that's about right."

"Coroner? Why a coroner? I thought they got involved only in deaths from other than natural causes?"

"Yes, that's right. It wasn't natural. He either committed suicide or was murdered."

If I had been shocked before, I was really thrown into a tizzy now. "Go slow there," I pleaded, "Tell me what happened—or seemed to have happened. I get the feeling this is going to get more than a little involved, and I'm going to end up somewhere in the middle before it's over."

"That's a pretty astute analysis," Jan said with a wry smile on her face. "The car that left a few minutes ago was the sheriff. He wanted to talk to you, but I sent him away. He'll be back in an hour or so. Go take a shower and I'll tell you what I know while you're getting dressed."

Jan sat on the chest at the foot of the bed while I towelled myself dry. "When Wing called, I thought it must be Rory's heart had finally given out. I don't think he had that much to drink, but alcohol mixed with the pure caffeine in those damned chocolate-covered beans Janie came up with is a deadly combination for anyone with a weak heart. That wasn't it however, although it helped. On the floor beside Rory's chair, I found a hypodermic needle and, then, a puncture wound in the vein of his left arm. I don't know what had been in the hypo, but can make a pretty good guess. When I showed the needle and puncture wound to Wing, she said, " 'Rory doesn't do drugs and neither do Mack or I. We smoke a joint now and then, but that's it.' I have no reason to doubt her."

"So you don't think it was suicide, do you?" I ran that around in my mind for a minute or two and came back to the other alternative. 'Why would anyone want to murder Rory?'

"Why, indeed. A lot of people around here don't care much for his life style, but not to the point of murder. Anyway, I called Chris and he called the sheriff."

I was dressed now. Still bewildered, I didn't know what to think. "Why do they want to talk to me?"

"As near as I can put it together, they're questioning everyone who was at the party. Somewhere along the way they've learned you drove Rory home. I guess Gary Grissom passed along that information and put you on the spot."

Yes, I thought, he would make sure the enforcement arm of the law had every available fact to work with. Next thing he would be offering to defend me. What was I thinking? "Defend me? Why would I need to be defended?" I blurted out.

"What are you talking about?" Jan asked with a startled look on her face.

"Oh, I don't know. I'm so confused. If Rory died at one o'clock, it must have happened just after I left him. If the sheriff knows that, he'll sure make me his prime suspect."

"Well, let's hope not, but brace yourself. I think he's back," Jan advised as we heard a car pull to a stop out front. Doors slammed and the doorbell rang.

The interview—it seemed more like a grilling to me—took place in the kitchen. All that was needed to make it complete was a sun lamp shining in my face. Jan sat us around the table and poured a mug of coffee for each of us. I almost spilled mine, but slopped only enough to make a small puddle on the Formica surface. I quickly dabbed it up with a napkin, but then didn't know what to do with the wet napkin. Jan reached over and took it from me.

"Now there, Missy, I'm Sheriff Branson and this is Officer Felton. We want to visit with you a little concerning what you know about last night. We're not going to make this all that formal; that is, we're not going to record our conversation, but Officer Felton here will make a few notes. Do you have any problem with that? If you want, you can call in a lawyer to counsel you."

"Lawyer? Why would I want a lawyer?"

"No reason, Missy. Don't fret. It's only fair that I advise you of that right."

He was a broad hulk of a man. His eyes had sort of a twinkle in them. His face was brown, seamed with wrinkles, and the corners of his mouth turned up as if he grinned a lot. He could have been somebody's grandfather and probably was. I calmed down—not much, but a little. I felt he would treat me gently.

"Now then, Missy, we've talked to a number of folks this morning, including the doctor here. We're trying to get everyone's recollections while they're still fresh in their minds. We're putting together a time line, sort of a calendar of events over the last day or so. We hope you can help us out with that."

I told my story of the evening as best I could recall it. So many people had been at the Cascade, it was hard to keep it and them straight. I told how Rory and I had met early in the evening, what we talked about as we sat at our table, what drinks he had and the food he ate. Much of this didn't seem to really interest Sheriff Branson, but he listened patiently as I rambled on. He brightened considerably when I got—finally, he probably thought—to the point of finding Rory slumped in the chair on the porch. He asked a few questions as I went on from there describing how Gary had helped me get Rory in the car, the drive to Rory's apartment, the climb up the stairs, and how he looked when I left. The only thing I didn't describe was the shadow beside the shed. I had concluded that was a quirk of my imagination and wasn't a vital or meaningful piece of information. I described the conversations Rory and I had during the half-hour or so before I left him in the apartment—or as close as I could remember them.

The most important thing (at least, I thought it was) was the plans Rory and I had made for the picnic on Sunday. "That was the very last thing we talked about. He was really looking forward to that."

"So then, Missy, what you're saying is you don't think he committed suicide. He was looking ahead. He wasn't ready to give up on everything. Is that it?"

"Yes. He really was. He wasn't looking back. For the moment, at least, he wasn't sad." I suddenly realized what I'd done. I'd ruled out suicide and left myself as the last person to have seen Rory alive. Or, next to the last, that is. I had, in effect, pointed the finger of fate directly at myself. What a dunce.

"Well then, Missy, that leaves us with just a short time between you closing the door and someone else opening it up to murder your friend. Now, just who do you suppose that could be? Who would have any reason to do such a thing?"

"I don't know. I hadn't seen Rory for twenty-five years. I don't know who were his friends or his enemies. I don't even know if he had any—enemies, that is." I knew I was in a hole and couldn't see any way out.

"Well then, Missy, if your friend was alone when you left, it's just possible someone was waiting for you to drive off, so he——or she——could get in there. Don't you think that could be? You didn't see anyone when you were leaving, did you?"

"No, I didn't, but I wasn't looking for anyone either." The business of that fleeting shadow kept nagging at me, but I still wasn't confident I had seen one. I decided not to mention it. Since I hadn't said anything about it in my summary of the events of the evening, the sheriff might think I was now making it up in order to draw suspicion away from myself. What was I thinking? If I was under suspicion, I had only myself to blame.

"Oh, Sheriff, there is something else. When I left Rory, I must have kept his key. He gave it to me when we first got to his room, but the door was unlocked. He said he must have forgotten to lock it. Anyway, here's the key. I don't know who else to give it to."

"Oh yes, Missy, we wondered where that had gotten to. I'll just take it along."

"I didn't realize you were looking for it. I didn't think it was that important."

"So then, Missy, I guess we'll just leave it at that for the time being. We do appreciate your cooperation. Thank you, Doctor, for the use of your kitchen and the coffee and such. The officer and I best be getting on."

With that, Officer Felton closed his notebook and stuck it in his back pocket. The two stood; the sheriff made a slight bow in my direction and they left. I heard car doors slam, the start of an engine, and its fading sound as they drove off. At least they didn't ring the siren. I hoped they hadn't turned on their flashing lights either.

Jan and I were silent for a few minutes. "It's a sad thing," she finally said. "He was a good kid. All the fault I found with him and my pleading to take better care of himself didn't add a single minute to his life."

"That may be," I replied, "but he knew you cared and that may have meant more than anything else. I don't think too many people really did care. It seemed to me he was treated like kind of an outcast, like he was from the other side of the tracks or something."

"We really should think about eating. It will soon be time to go to the school. I thought earlier I wouldn't go, but we should. Rory wouldn't want us to pass that up because of him. And, you haven't been there in so long, it would be a shame for you not to go."

I merely nodded my head. Yes, she was right, as usual. "I still can't understand why he just sat there and let someone, even a friend, stick a needle in his arm. That really doesn't make sense."

"That wasn't the way it was. Until you left, Rory was probably navigating on nerve alone. The minute you closed the door, it all caught up with him. I know what kind of shape his heart was in and I have a pretty good idea of the amount of alcohol and caffeine he had in his system. I think it hit him all at once. Quite frankly, I believe he was almost dead when whoever it was gave him that hypo. If something was needed to push him over the edge, that was it, but I don't think it was necessary. In my opinion, if the murderer had waited another fifteen minutes or so, he wouldn't have had to become one. Nature would have accomplished the same thing with a lot less trouble than is ahead of us now."

I was somewhat relieved at that pronouncement. As a layperson, I was in no position to argue with a medical professional about death or the imminence of it. I felt a little less guilty about the fact I had, in effect, left Rory to his fate without doing something to alter it. I guessed it was inevitable if Jan said so and nothing I could have done would have changed the result.

It was just after one o'clock when Jan and I climbed the long, winding sidewalk and flights of concrete steps to the front door of the school. The last flight, just beyond the driveway, led to a landing in front of three, heavy, wooden doors. Indeed, they were heavy. As I dawdled along one day, this same door closed on my foot and almost severed it or, at least, that's how it felt. This was the traditional site where classes posed for group pictures for the annual yearbook. Just inside, on opposite walls of the vestibule hung framed lists of each graduating class. Once, the Class of '68 had been at the end of the top row; now it was so far down the line, it took a search to find it.

The marble floors of the long halls shown—I supposed the custodial staff had worked extra hard and long to make the place presentable for the reminiscent visitors they expected. We looked in at the grade rooms arrayed along one side of the hall as we walked toward the stairs. When we were in those rooms we had dreamed of the time we would finally be old enough to move to the second floor where the "big kids" were. It seemed like a never-ending journey, room by room, grade by grade, from one end of the school to the other until, at last, we climbed those stairs to the level of higher learning. We had become grownups, we thought, only to learn we had regressed to the low rung of the ladder, looked down upon by everyone from freshmen to seniors. Being in the seventh grade had turned out to be not that great a climb after all.

Jan and I climbed the stairs again. We looked in at the science lab on the right and the cafeteria before turning left. The hall was filled with former students all saying the same thing, "Remember when. . ." Nostalgia rolled back the years. We saw some of our classmates and waved. Jan went over to speak with someone. I didn't notice who it was. I looked far down the long hall and saw a tall boy with touseled red hair striding along. It could have been Rory, but I knew it wasn't. I looked again and he was still there walking toward me, but not getting any closer. He seemed to be yelling something to me as he pointed over his shoulder. Then I saw a dark figure behind him, but couldn't make out any face. I wanted to ask Rory who it was, who he was pointing at, but I couldn't make a sound. Suddenly, I felt a hand on my shoulder. I screamed.

Everyone stopped talking and looked at me. Who could blame them? "Sorry," a voice said. "I didn't mean to startle you." I turned, slowly and full of dread, to see who was there. It was Gary Grissom. "I saw you and wanted to tell you Syd came in this morning. He was asking about you."

"No, I'm the one who's sorry, Gary. I was daydreaming. I must have been a million miles away." I looked down the long hallway. The red-headed boy was no longer there. Neither was the dark figure that had been pursuing him. It all must have been my imagination, like the shadow behind the shed. Was I really seeing things or what?

Jan appeared at my side clearly irate. "Gary Grissom, what are you doing to this girl? She's been through a lot this morning. She doesn't need someone to scare her out of her wits."

"I didn't do anything. Nothing," he protested, backing away.

I tried to straighten out the situation. "He's right, he didn't do anything. I thought I saw .... I thought .... Oh, I don't know what I thought."

That sure went a long way toward making sense out of my own foolishness. However, it must have assured those around us. The hubbub in the hall picked up where it had been just before my outburst. Alumni, old and young alike, resumed their pursuit of youth by looking in the rooms and trying to recall long-forgotten combinations to the lockers on the opposite wall. More than one was thrilled to remember the number they had used and to find it still there. I wasn't one of those; I thought the lockers had been farther down the hall.

The three of us—Jan, Gary, and I—went down to the end of the hall and were pleased to see the door to the library standing open. This had been my favorite place in the whole school. Molly Cornwall and I had spent hours there, studying and whispering across the table when we thought Mrs. Griffen wouldn't notice. As we went in, I looked around thinking I would see Molly already there, but she wasn't. I knew Mrs. Griffen had retired years ago and died soon after. Mostly, I thought, because her life had ended the day she walked out of this room for the last time. I didn't recognize the girl (she was much younger than I, so that made her a girl) who stood next to the desk. She was obviously the current librarian, they were always easy to pick out in a crowd.

We sat at one of the round tables. The silence rule had obviously been canceled for the day because most of the visitors were doing just that, visiting. I expected to hear the rap of a pencil and a shush for quiet, but neither happened although the librarian looked ill at ease and was finding it difficult to countenance all the noise in her sanctum sanctorum. The expression on her face said she'd be glad when this day was over.

"I really didn't mean to scare you," Gary again apologized. "I should have spoken first. I should have realized how upset you must be. I guess you were the last to see Rory alive."

Jan was quick to correct that. "What are you talking about? We know someone else came along after El left."

"Yes, yes, I know. What I meant was, she was the last one to see him before someone else murdered him. I guess everyone has concluded that's what happened." Turning to me he said, "I would have sat in with you when the sheriff interviewed you this morning if you had wanted."

"I know that, Gary, but I didn't think I needed any help. Besides, Jan was there and the sheriff was only interested in the events of the evening. He wasn't accusing me, or anyone else, of anything. Or, so he said."

We talked some more, trying to change the subject, but it didn't work. We had only one thing an our minds. In the end, we agreed to meet at the banquet that evening. Gary left and Jan and I went down the stairs next to the library and out the side door of the building. Revisiting the past hadn't been as rejuvenating as I had hoped.

The real reunion took place in the huge room beyond the bar in the main lodge at the ski center. The annual event had always been there so Jan said. It was, after all, the only local place large enough to hold the crowd that came each year. The parking lot was rapidly filling when we arrived. I drove the Buick. Emma would have wanted me to flash it in front of my old friends. However, none of them happened to arrive at the same time, so it was a wasted effort.

It was a huge building. Even after all these years it seemed big. I had worked in the cafeteria on winter weekends my last two years at Plainview High, as did almost half the students at the school. Without that place to work most of us would have been idle. My brother had worked in the parking lot directing cars to line up in what were supposed to be neat, orderly rows, but ended up looking like a serpent writhing across the lot. He and his partner always seemed to be missing when they were most needed. I dreaded hearing his name blared over the public address system directing them to report to their station. Whenever that happened, all my coworkers looked at me and shrugged their shoulders as if to say they weren't surprised. Why the manager kept the two of them on the payroll, I'll never know.

The tables for the Class of '68 were right where Patty had said they would be and she was too. She waved us on when we turned the corner at the end of the bar, which was, as might be expected, already doing a land-office business. The four bartenders looked like they would have welcomed an increase in staffing.

Being one of the honored classes and the biggest of the two (a relative term,the fifty-year group would surely have lost more members at this point in history), we would more than fill our corner of the room. Most of those who had been at the get-together the evening before were there as were others who had arrived that day. Syd Kaplan hadn't changed much. Like the rest of us, he was older and had put on a few pounds. He probably could still have played the first quarter of a basketball game, but would have faded after that. We hugged and said how glad we were to see each other and really meant it. He introduced me to his wife, whom I hadn't met before. Of course, I was subjected to the inevitable photographs of the twins, both sets. The older two were now in college and the younger ones were juniors in high school. I looked skyward (or ceilingward in the domed room) and raised up a thank you for having been allowed that long-ago trip down I-95 and the way out of what would have been a frustrating marriage.

Patty checked us in. I think we were the only class that had attendance taken. However, bless her heart, she had made black armbands and passed them out as each class member arrived. It was a thoughtful gesture and others of us should have had the same idea. Rory would have been pleased to see those expressions of remembrance. As I pulled mine up over my elbow, I had the horrid thought that maybe, just maybe, one person wearing an armband that night might be the reason they were necessary.

Of course, the alumni association had a president and he soon called the assembled masses to order. It took a while to get everyone seated. No one was in a hurry, except the bartenders, who were probably relieved at this slight respite. Their services would surely be required throughout the long evening, but the pace would be more manageable.

The order of events was nothing out of the ordinary. The usual grace was spoken by a local pastor, who turned out to be a 1975 graduate of Plainview High. A retired army sergeant (another graduate) led the pledge of allegiance. We sang the Alma Mater. Patty's handouts weren't needed; the words were printed on the back of the programs. That was followed by introductions of the head table and of honored guests scattered about the room. Many soon lost interest and a low buzz developed as conversations picked up at most of the tables.

Seating had been random. Why Patty hadn't come up with place cards and a well-thought-out seating plan was a surprise to most of us. I ended up between Jan on my left and Jamie Timmerman. He had introduced me to his wife the evening before, but I didn't remember her name. She hadn't been a local girl and, if he had told me where she came from and why, I had forgotten.

"I'm honored to be sitting next to the mayor," I smiled to open the conversation.

"Well, don't be," Jamie laughed. Still had perfect teeth I saw and also noticed his glass was filled with plain cola, which was a switch from what I remembered of him. "We used to sit next to each other in math class. I always made sure of that so I could look over at your answers on those awful quizzes old Kitteredge—whoops, Mr. Kitteredge—used to give us every Friday."

Yes, I did remember math class, although I never thought I did well enough to have my answers copied. "You should have sat next to Rory. He usually aced every math test he took."

"Isn't that a fact. He was a lot better student than most people remember. He seemed to be dreaming about something else—fishing, more than likely—until the teacher asked a question trying to catch him not paying attention. They were always surprised, but shouldn't have been, when he came up with the right answer. I'm going to miss seeing him around town."

We talked, off and on, throughout the evening to the person next to us, across the table, over at the next table. We stopped to listen—

really listen, that is—to what was going on only when Molly—easily the most famous and accomplished person in our class—went up to represent us. In her speech, which was mercifully shorter that any of the rest, she explained the reason we were wearing black armbands and asked for a minute of silence in memory of our lost classmate. It was the only quiet moment of the night.

Jan and I didn't stay for the dancing. Being without escort, we would have looked like the wallflowers we really were. Some guy—I never did figure out who he was and Jan didn't know him either—wandered around all evening with a video camera. He passed out his card to everyone he shot saying the cost of a tape of the whole event, speeches and all, would be $50 and could be ordered in about a month. I took his card, but still didn't recognize him even when I read his name. While I didn't think I would want a tape for myself, I thought maybe Roger and Emma would enjoy watching it. And maybe not.

Oh, yes, I did see Uncle Harry and Aunt Sarah. They spotted me before I saw them. Or, at least, Aunt Sarah did. The first I knew they were there was when I heard her strident voice, "Holy shit, Harry, there's Ellyn." Truly, then, I was home again.

EIGHT

THE COUNTRY AIR agreed with me. The sun was high when I awoke; its brightness wasn't completely shut out by the drapes at the window. Actually, it wasn't the sun that woke me from a deep, dream-free sleep. It was a rapping at the door and Jan's voice asking, "Are you going to lay abed all day in there, Sleepyhead?"

I struggled awake, taking a minute or two to realize where I was. Then, reality struck and I remembered why I was here and the tragedy I was part of. I hoped the reason Jan was getting me up and around wasn't as traumatic and sad as had greeted us the morning before. Apprehensive, I splashed some water on my face, brushed my teeth, ran a brush through my hair, and hurried down the hall to the kitchen. I was relieved when I saw Jan sitting calmly at the table with a smile on her face.

"It's a beautiful day. Just the kind one would wish for if a picnic was on the agenda."

Oh, my, yes, the picnic. If today's the picnic, it must be Sunday. "Can we wait until I have some coffee before we leave?" I pleaded, hoping we wouldn't have to head for the lake until noon or so.

She laughed as she placed a cup of steaming coffee in front of me. "Yeah, we can hold off a while. I just didn't want you to miss this late spring morning. The birds are singing, a fresh breeze is blowing, the flowers are coloring the countryside, and the grass is growing, which reminds me. I'd better call Jason to make sure he shows up tomorrow morning to mow the lawn. You don't know Jason. He's one of Dan and Dolly's brood."

We talked about a lot of things, both of us evading the subject most on our minds. The reunion of the evening before had been pleasant, but Rory's death and the fact he had been murdered muted any celebration we might have planned and it became——for the Class of '68 anyway——a subdued affair. I was glad it was over, but looked forward to the picnic. The crowd would be much smaller and we would each know who all the others were. Well, not everyone. I had no hope I would ever get it straight who was who's wife or husband or what child went with which set of parents. The picnic was to be a family kind of thing. Kids of all ages were welcome as long as they belonged to someone from the class. North Lake and the state land around it would provide plenty of space for them to roam.

The telephone rang. Jan reached for the extension on the counter next to the table. "I hope it's not the hospital telling me one of my patients has just been brought into the emergency room."

It wasn't. The conversation was mostly one-sided. Jan kept nodding her head and made notes on the pad she kept ready beside the phone.

"That was the coroner. He's an old friend. He said Rory died of cardiac arrhythmia. He found traces of cocaine in Rory's blood and urine and that, coupled with his heart condition, caused his death. The cocaine was introduced into his system by injection into a vein on his left arm. His tests on the hypodermic needle determined it had held a cocaine solution."

She put the pad on the table. The notes she had made while talking on the phone were a sad obituary for an old friend. We looked at each other and were silent for a minute or two. Finally, I asked, "Could Rory have been using drugs? It seems hard to believe anyone would want to kill him."

"If he had been using drugs, I would have known it. Oh I'm sure he experimented twenty and more years ago just like a lot of others, but since I've been taking care of him——and that's been at least ten years——he hasn't."

I still couldn't accept that Rory had been murdered. On the other hand, I couldn't believe he would commit suicide. But he was gone and, with the coroner's report, it had to be one or the other. Either choice was a bad one as far as I was concerned.

Consulting the notes on the pad, Jan went on, "The coroner said he and the sheriff have released the body and he thinks the funeral will be on Tuesday."

All I could think of was that meant our class would have one more opportunity to get together. It was something we could have done without. As each hour passed, I wondered more and more if I should have come to the reunion. How calm and quiet—well, comparatively, that is—everything was in Cal's Corner. I never should have left it.

Jan, reading my mind, interrupted my thoughts, "It wouldn't have made any difference if you hadn't come. Whatever the reason for what has happened, it wasn't because you were here."

"Oh, I hope you're right. I just feel so bad and kind of guilty, but I don't know why."

-- 0 --

Unlike the Adirondack Mountains to the north and the state of Minnesota, the Catskills are not a land of lakes, 10,000 or any other great number. They are, instead, the land of few—darned few—lakes and the biggest of these are the man-made reservoirs that inundated whole valleys and the villages, farms, and communities within them in order to store water to satisfy the thirsty millions in faraway New York City. Of the few natural lakes in the Catskills, most are owned by the state and many of these were enlarged and the water level raised by building dams across the outlet streams.

North Lake is located on the eastern escarpment of the Catskills, not far from Plainview and is the site of one of the earliest public campgrounds in the state. The entire of the lake and over 2,000 acres of surrounding land were acquired by the State of New York in 1930 and the site was developed (in complete contravention of the "forever wild" clause in the state's constitution, my father always preached to anyone and everyone who would listen) into a campsite complete with gravel roads, fireplaces, picnic tables, latrines, and a water supply system. It opened for public use in 1931.

Over the decades following, the state made a number of additional acquisitions to expand the public lands around the site.Not long after the North Lake purchase, the state acquired a 600-acre tract on the westerly slopes of South Mountain down to and including the hairpin turn on the highway that snaked down the mountain toward the flat lands of the Hudson Valley. Land east of that parcel and extending to the site of the old Kaaterskill Hotel that perched (before it burned, that is) near the summit of the mountain was purchased in 1933.

In 1961, the state acquired a 10-acre parcel in back of the beach area of North Lake. This small parcel had been parted off the Catskill Mountain House property in 1953 to be turned into a tourist attraction called Rip's Retreat. In fact, it was so close to the beach that the refreshment stand on the Retreat property was built with the back of the building on the line between the public and private lands. The top half of the back wall could be opened so campsite patrons could buy hot dogs and such on that side of the building while visitors to the Retreat made their purchases from the front of the building. The attraction featured old Rip Van Winkle and his dog wandering about while gnomes toiling in little cabins made wooden shoes, blew glass trinkets, and crafted other period gimcracks. For an extra dollar or two, visitors to the Retreat could take a ride in an old wagon pulled by a team of horses driven by a voluble local character down to Rip Van Winkle Hollow (formerly called Sleepy Hollow), the site of Rip's Rock (where he supposedly slept those twenty years) and the one-time location of Rip Van Winkle House, a stop on the old coach road leading up to the Mountain House.

In 1962, the last 259 acres of the Catskill Mountain House property passed into state ownership. The world-famous hotel that faced the open ledge overlooking the Hudson had once been host to presidents and generals, actors and writers, people of renown and just plain folks, including my Aunt Cal. One of her favorite stories was of her visit there while in her late teens. She never forgot the eight-course meal she was served in the spacious dining room. It was a fine summer day near the turn of the century when she and her beau journeyed there by train. She was treated like royalty, she said; it was an experience to be remembered.

However, by the 1960s, the halcyon days were over for the Catskill Mountain House. The rambling structure had decayed to a dangerous state. Windows were broken; walls tilted in all directions ready to fall, it seemed, in a gentle breeze; floors were rotten with boards missing; parts of the roof had fallen in. The once-magnificent portico had originally been graced by thirteen ornate columns spaced evenly across the front. All but three of these were gone and the roof overhead, crumbling also, was supported by wooden poles. In the dark of the early morning of January 25, 1963, residents under the mountain were startled to see a red glow lighting the western sky. The New York State Conservation Department burned the once-proud and majestic hostelry to the ground. It was an ignominious finish to a symbol of a bygone era but, perhaps, a fitting end—it went out in a blaze of glory.

Also in 1962, the state acquired the entire of South Lake and this provided for a doubling of the facilities of the campsite. In time, the dam on the lower lake was rebuilt to raise the water level of the lakes. In effect, this construction by the department's mound builders, as my father called them, made one lake out of the two. What had been a small stream joining them became a water wide enough to be easily navigated by canoes and rowboats. In the process, with scant attention to history, the department destroyed one of the corners of the Hardenburgh Patent. In 1787, John Cox, running the north line of the patent, set a pile of stones on the bank of the stream connecting North and South Lakes. When the stream channel was widened at the time of raising the dam, the pile of stones was cast aside, unnoticed and unlamented by those overwhelmed by an uncontrollable need for what they called progress.

In 1965, the state's acquisition program culminated with the purchase of the Laurel House property. This hotel was another imposing structure that featured something the famous Mountain House didn't have. It was perched on the edge of a deep ravine into which plunged Kaaterskill Falls, said to be the highest and most scenic east of the Mississippi River. The stream creating them was the outlet of South Lake. Beyond the falls, the stream tumbled steeply down the ravine, over Bastion Falls just above the hairpin turn, and on down to join Kaaterskill Creek to flow out of the Clove and beyond to the Hudson. The Laurel House struggled on until 1964. Its brochure for that season boasted the return of "our Continental Chef," the "new Rhythmic Band" that would play in "our Beautiful Large Ballroom," and "our Very Own—Our Beautiful Kaaterskill Waterfall, where you can find the most Legendary and Romantic Atmosphere in the Whole State of New York." Not long after the purchase by the state, this relic of days past went the way of its near neighbor, the Mountain House. It, too, was burned by the state.

-- 0 --

I had seen the Mountain House in its dilapidated condition and then had trouble envisioning the grandeur experienced by Aunt Cal. I had missed the Laurel House in my travels and was probably the only person in the Catskills who had never seen Kaaterskill Falls. That had been part of the itinerary of the hike Rory and I had planned for the day of the picnic. Now, that was not to be and I would probably leave this world without ever seeing that wonder of nature.

Jan had no idea what was planned for the picnic—food, entertainment, or otherwise. She had been involved in the Friday night get-together and the reunion, but had begged off at a third request from Patty. "I'm sure she's found some willing soul to keep busy," she said as we started out in the early afternoon. "We're supposed to be there at twelve, but let's be like high society and be late for a change."

I thought the analogy to high society was a bit of a reach. I didn't know anyone in that class, but from what I did know, I couldn't imagine too many of them going to a picnic at North Lake. We did, however, go in the Buick, just in case anyone had missed seeing me driving around in it before. Even that impression was lost when Jan pointed out the sticker on the back bumper advising everyone to "Call 1-800-624-4660 to reserve an Avis car of your choice."

The drive was a short one; the campsite was only a few miles from Plainview. I hadn't been there in years and was surprised to reach the gate house some distance before we got to the point where I remembered the entrance to be. The next surprise was a young (at least, young to me) girl in a ranger uniform complete with one of those wide-brimmed Smoky Bear hats. However, one could have forgiven her officialness when she replied to our query for directions. "Oh, you girls must be part of the reunion. Just take the road to the left and follow it around to the far side of the lake. Have a good time." Girls. Well, I guess.

Road was the word for it. It was macadam all the way. My father would have turned around and left had he been with us and would have been even more aghast at the flush toilets not far from the pavilion we were assigned. A crowd was there and an old tune was being played by three musicians set up off to one side. Not unexpectedly, Patty was there to greet us.

"I thought must be a patient had delayed you when you weren't here at noon. Bernie asked three of his band people to come along to keep us entertained. Isn't that great?"

Jan rolled her eyes, but agreed it was just great. Patty pointed out where the snacks and cold drinks were. "We can go swimming if you want to. Remember I said to bring your suits."

I hadn't remembered that being one of the recommendations in the material I had received so long ago and probably wouldn't have brought my suit even if I had. I certainly didn't want old friends who remembered what I looked like in a bathing suit twenty-five years ago to see me in one now. Jan and I were both surprised when Patty didn't give us name tags or some other handout. "Must be she thinks we know each other by now," we said at the same time.

I had expected the picnic to be a somber affair, but it wasn't. This was mostly because of the progeny of my classmates. These included late teenagers, some of whom were obviously in love and spent the afternoon strolling hand in hand along the paths of the campsite while gazing dreamily into each other's eyes. Would you believe it, some grandchildren were there as well ranging from toddlers to mere babes in arms. One of these looked to me to have been born on the way to the picnic, but was actually two weeks old. As at some family reunions, I wondered if we were going to announce the oldest and the youngest in attendance. The two-week-old tiny tot was obviously the youngest and, after looking over the crowd, I decided I was the oldest or, at least, felt that way.

I wandered up the slope to the site of the Mountain House and, in the words of some poet I couldn't recall, "the view hence was magnificent." Nothing remained of the hotel or of the other buildings that had made up the complex. The site was leveled out to the ledge and was marked by a large metal sign telling the story of the Mountain House in concise wording of raised letters. Of course, a number of thoughtless tourists had, with some difficulty, scratched their names into the hard surface as if trying to secure a place in history; they succeeded only in marring the legend of the place.

I could see the Hudson far off and realized the old story of the illusion one experienced while looking at it was true. Supposedly, the first hunter who arrived at the spot centuries before said he put a round pebble in the barrel of his flintlock and aimed it at the river. When he did, the pebble rolled back and hit him in the eye proving, just as he had thought, the Hudson River was higher than the ledge on which he stood. Indeed, as I looked at the river, I had the sensation I was looking up at it instead of down.

I could hear the sounds of the picnic. The music was good; the old songs recalled forgotten thoughts. The inevitable softball game had started and I could hear the clank of horseshoes. I walked back toward the pavilion and paused when it came into view. People—good friends—were scattered about, talking, eating, laughing. I looked at each of them and asked myself—Who? Who? And why?

NINE

THE MORNING AFTER THE PICNIC, I was sitting in the little parlor, drinking coffee, when Chris Rafferty appeared at the French doors. I waved to him, gesturing they were open. He came in, took off his hat and tossed in on the sofa. Looking around questionably, he finally decided that piece of furniture was the most comfortable and joined the hat.

"Do you want some coffee?" I asked. "Or tea? Or something? Bagel?" I held up the one I had been nibbling on.

He shook his head. "I was wondering if I could ask you a couple of questions." It wasn't really a request.

"Of course. Why not?" I answered. "Are you sure you don't want something? We have juice, I think."

"I'm fine," he said, fishing a small spiral notebook from his pocket. He looked kind of like Joe Friday on Dragnet. He also didn't act all that happy. "Look, I have to ask you these things——for the, you know, investigation." He looked awfully ill at ease.

"Go ahead," I said. What on earth was the matter?

"Now, you were the last person to see Rory alive, is that right?"

"Well, I guess. Except for the killer."

"Right." I heard skepticism in his voice. I got up and walked over to the sofa. I stood in front of him and looked down. I could see he was beginning to lose his hair. "Chris, what's this all about? Am I a suspect?"

His voice was calm, maybe a little too calm. "Would you mind returning to your seat, please?"

"Chris? Return to my seat, please? That sounds like bad dialogue from a bad movie. You know I didn't have anything to do with Rory's death." I paused. "Don't you?" Oh my God, I thought, I come to a reunion and now I'm going to spend the rest of my life in Attica. Do they have women in Attica? It didn't make any difference; I'd end up in some ghastly place. Emma's golden memories would consist of seeing my face through a layer of plexiglass and hearing my voice on the telephone. I wondered if they would let me out to attend her graduation. I realized my original instincts were correct. I should never have come to this stupid thing.

Chris was looking at me, holding his pen above the notebook. "We have a little problem. We need to clear up this thing about the key."

I was getting a little irritated. "What thing about what key?"

"You had his apartment key?" This sounded like a statement, but was actually a question.

"Yes, I did have his key. I asked him for it so I could open the door to help him in."

"How did that happen? That you needed to ask him for the key, I mean?"

"Chris, you were right there. He had a lot to drink and wasn't feeling well besides that. We all agreed----Gary and Rory and I, that is----that he shouldn't drive his motorcycle, so I took him home. You know all that."

"So how did you happen to have the key the next morning?"

I felt like kicking him in the shins. "Chris, for Pete's sake. I took him back to his room. As you know, he could hardly walk. I asked him for his key and he gave it to me. When we realized the door wasn't locked, I stuck it in my pocket and then helped him inside. We talked a few minutes and, since he didn't seem to want me to stay, I left. I simply forgot to give him back his key. The next morning, Wing found him." My voice sort of trailed off, remembering the way Rory had looked when I closed the door.

"Why is everyone so concerned about that key?" I went on.

"Because it's the only key to Rory's place and you told Sheriff Branson you locked the door behind you when you left."

Well, I had to admit that was a good reason, but didn't say so. Chris was watching me, although not in the way you would look at someone you had known for forty years and who had, in third grade, hit you over the head with a clipboard. He was looking at me in the way you look at a person you think may have committed a murder.

"Had you had any recent contact with the victim?"

That was scary. Rory had gone from friend to victim. I had gone from friend to suspect. "Do I need a lawyer?" I asked. My voice sounded funny, even to me.

"Not yet."

NOT YET. That was encouraging. I guess he meant I could call my lawyer after he read me the Miranda warnings. It didn't matter anyway because my lawyer was a thousand miles away and up till now all he had ever done for me was write my will and ask me to sign a bunch of papers at the closing when we bought the house.

Chris was looking at me expectantly. I knew he had asked me a question, but I couldn't remember what it was. "What did you say?"

"I asked if you had had any recent contact with the victim?"

"The only contact we had since graduation was the other night at the party, although I did send him a Christmas card one year long ago. I think I sent you one that year, too. And, as I remember it, you didn't send me one back."

"Did he respond?"

"Chris, this is ridiculous. It was just a card. It said, 'Merry Christmas and Happy New Year,' or something like that. Surely, you know about Christmas cards. I probably wrote a little note about some funny thing that had happened in school and that was that. I hadn't seen him again until this weekend."

"But you have spoken to him."

I wondered how he knew that. "Yes, I did talk to him on the phone a few weeks ago. He got my number from Jan and called me. He just wanted to know if I was coming to the reunion. When I said I was, he said he wanted to talk to me when I got here. I don't know what about. He didn't say."

"Chris," I went on, sitting on the very edge of my chair—or seat, as he had called it. "You have known me practically all your life. I remember the time you wet your pants in the first grade." I shouldn't have mentioned that but I was really agitated at this point. "I did not kill Rory Hale and you know it."

Chris took a deep breath. I waited as he considered his reply. I was hoping that whatever his plans were for the immediate future, they didn't include handcuffs.

"El, you have to understand. I'm Chief of Police in this town. It's a small town and I've lived here all my life. Just about every time I give somebody a ticket, or stop a drunk driver, or respond to domestic violence, I'm dealing with someone I've known, and probably been friends with for a long time. I can't take that into consideration. I have to ask you these things. The sheriff is doing both of us a favor by letting me question you, as it is. You were the last person known to have seen the victim alive. You had his room key. Not only that, you had the only room key and you said you locked the door behind you when you left. How do I know you didn't administer the hypodermic needle?"

"For one thing, Jan got in not long after I came home. I was already here. That didn't leave enough time for me to do what you think I did. You should ask her about that."

"I plan to."

Terrific. He was checking out my story. "For the second thing. What reason could I possibly have for killing Rory? I hadn't seen him in decades. I don't know anything about his life other than what Jan told me. Why would I kill him? Because he made honor society a year before I did?" In my mind, I saw myself being arrested by the police, played by Chris, while my lawyer, played by Gary, defended me to the press. I wondered how often they allowed visiting at the state prison. I wondered if they would let me wear earrings. I wondered why in the world I had ever returned to this town. Maybe none of this is real, I thought. Maybe this is some bizarre practical joke. Maybe it's April Fool's Day. Maybe (please God, I don't ask for much) I was on Candid Camera.

Chris closed his notebook. "Is there anything you remember about the night of the murder that might be helpful? Anything at all, no matter how strange it might seem to you."

"I think I've already told you everything I know. Nothing out of the ordinary happened," I said, in kind of a shrill voice. "Except, of course, for Rory being dead when I woke up the next morning."

Chris stood and put the notebook in his pocket. "You know where I am, if you do think of anything." He started out, then turned and looked at me. "Anything at all." He closed the French doors behind him.

I burst into Jan's office, where I found her scribbling something in a patient's chart. "What is the matter with you?" she asked. She looked at me. "Are you okay?"

I sat in one of the chairs in front of her desk. "Oh yeah, I'm fine. Just peachy. I'm on my way to prison, but other than that everything is going just swimmingly. So glad you asked."

"What in the world are you talking about?"

"Chris has been over here asking me a bunch of stupid questions about Rory's death. He thinks I killed him."

"I don't believe he thinks you killed him." I realized Chris's visit wasn't exactly a surprise to Jan. "I think he thinks you might have seen something that seems insignificant to you, but is really important."

I told myself there was a little bit of irony in this. Before I left Georgia, I was mildly disappointed I hadn't accomplished much with my life. Now it seemed highly possible I would achieve my fifteen minutes of fame on the arm of a burly bailiff.

"Also," Jan went on, "It does seem a little suspicious that you had the only key to his apartment."

I was flabbergasted. "You know there was nothing suspicious about it. It just happened. Anyway, that can't be the only key to that place. There must be extra keys, a master key, stuff like that."

I leaned back in the chair. It was leather. "I'm sure there are." Jan's voice was very soothing. This was probably the voice she used when she told people they had cancer with only two months to live. She put her hands on the desk and pushed her chair back. She stood and came around to where I was sitting. "Come on," she said. "Let's go bake some brownies."

Well, that was more like it. We left the office, side by side, and it seemed like only yesterday we were in this very house making a mess in the kitchen. We made another one.

As the time for it drew closer, I approached Tuesday's funeral with a feeling of dread, but this should have come as no surprise. I can't imagine anyone enjoying those things, not even undertakers. In my case though, it would create a double sense of loss. Sure, Rory was gone and this would say farewell to him. In addition, I had come to the reunion with the idea of updating my memory, so to speak. My recollections of my classmates were not much more than images. In some cases, these were one-dimensional; all I had were pictures in a yearbook. I had wanted to see real, talking, walking, people----albeit with a few years added on----to replace those faded remembrances. Now I would leave----if I left at all----not with memories of smiling, laughing faces, but of sad, grieving faces and maybe even a tear or two. It wasn't fair, I thought, the visions of good times planned had been dashed by the senseless act of some unknown player in the game of life----or of death.

My mother came. We had talked on the telephone every day I had been in the mountains. Rory had been in her cub scout den those many years ago and, along with all the other boys, had severely tried her patience at times, but they all remembered her fondly and she them. She had wondered if perhaps the three of us could go together. We had a cup of tea in the little parlor, reminisced a bit, and talked as mothers and daughters----and friends----do.

The funeral was in the undertaking home instead of a church. Which one----church, that is----would have been a difficult choice. Rory was about as non-denominational as one could get. I don't think he questioned the reality of a God; he was too much attuned to the natural world to not believe some greater being had put it together. If he had worshipped, it had been at the altar of a trout stream, of the nod of a woodland flower in the breeze, of the song of a bird. It was fitting that spring had taken over the hills and fleecy clouds dotted the blue sky on this day.

His mother and father were there. Their marriage had fallen apart years before, but they came together this once to mourn the passing of the one tangible remains of it. Whomever had chosen the bearers had stayed with the Class of '68. Since it was the time of its reunion, the thought was appropriate. Gary Grissom, Chris Rafferty, and Jamie Timmerman were logical choices; here were three of the local group, those who had stayed with or returned to the scenes of their youth. David Solomon, Syd Kaplan, and Micheal Blake represented those who had thought the wide world offered a better chance for success and had gone out there to find it. I looked at each one and tried to remember who of them had been Rory's best friend and suddenly realized I had.

The back rows were filled with a later group of friends. At first, they seemed out of place, but the more I thought about it, I concluded that, perhaps, we were the ones who should have stepped aside so they could claim the right to be closest to the one in the casket. They wore black leather jackets and boots, a few were bedecked with silver chains, some had their hair in braided pony tails, others were bald or getting close to it. I picked out Wing and Mack among them. These were the bikers; Rory would have been pleased to see so many there.

The service was short and most everyone was glad of that. I had wondered about joining the line passing the open casket, but my mother took my elbow and urged me along. I paused and looked down at him. He looked natural, but that's a standard remark at all funerals and doesn't really say much. I was pleased to see that some thoughtful soul—his mother, probably—had placed his fishing pole beside him. As I turned to move on, it seemed—it really did—it seemed as if Rory was trying to tell me something. I looked again, but nothing had moved or changed.

The procession to the cemetery was a noisy affair, but not out of place. The bikers lined up directly in back of the hearse, forming in ranks of three. They had appointed themselves as honor guard and no one stepped forward to deny them the privilege. I could think of no reason why one would want to. The roar of that phalanx of machines was enough to wake the dead, but didn't. It wasn't that long of a ride—only about four miles or so—to the solemn, greenswarded, rural cemetery set back from the road and partially hidden in the trees, but folks for miles around must have heard us as we slowly wound our way there. The roar echoed back and forth from the surrounding hills. It was an anthem Rory would have liked.

The grave site was at the back of the cemetery, on the bluff above a stream that coursed on its way to join the upper reaches of the Schoharie. I hoped it held a few trout. Molly Cornwall spoke lovingly about how Rory had been such an important part of our years in school and that closed the grave-side ceremony.

It was probably the last time I would see many of the people there. As we milled around saying our good-byes, we vowed to come together again at our fiftieth reunion. We all knew, however, that some of us would surely be gone by then. We also knew we probably wouldn't "Keep in touch" in the meantime or "Stop in" whenever we passed through this state or that. I should have been sad or depressed, but found I was relieved. No matter what the future held, I was glad the reunion was over, really over. While it was good to see everyone again even with the tragedy that had come into our midst, we each had separate lives now and were anxious to get back to them.

My mother, Jan, and I went through the Clove and beyond to Al's in Phoenicia. This had been a favorite restaurant when my brother and I were growing up. The place hadn't changed much, but the staff were all new faces to me—except for Sally, that is—but Jan seemed to know them all. We raised our glasses in memory of Rory, wishing him rest and peace. While neither of us said so, we each wondered what would be the answer to the question we all had in our minds.

TEN

IT WAS LATE THE NEXT MORNING before I finally put myself together and was ready to go. I went down the hall to Jan's office to tell her I was leaving and to remind her I would be back to spend the last couple of days with her before returning home. She was with a patient in the examining room, so I left a note in the middle of her desk. I wondered how she kept it so neat and tidy; mine certainly wasn't.

The drive to my mother's house was only about ten miles, but I remembered how much longer it seemed on my first day of kindergarten. The yellow school bus was so very big and the steps into it were so high I didn't think I could make it. My mother helped me surmount that obstacle every morning that year. The next year I was in the first grade and big enough (or so I thought) to get along on my own. That ride had seemed like a trip around the world to me and, considering the smallness of my world back then, I guess it was. I thought we'd never get to school that first day. When we did, I was almost too scared to get off the bus. Fortunately, I wasn't the only one who was ready to defer entrance into the adventurous world of learning. Another little girl was standing hesitantly in front of the huge front door of the school and was obviously as scared as I. We looked at each other and, without saying anything, joined hands and went in together. Jan and I had been the best of friends from that moment on.

My mother had lunch all ready. It was tomato soup and egg salad sandwiches, my all-time favorite when I was little. On lonely days yet, when nothing seems to go the way I expect, that's what I make for myself. She had a table set on the inside/outside porch. At least, that's what one of my brother's friends had once called it and the designation stuck. It was a little room off the kitchen, screened across one side, and looked out on the cool, back yard, which was marked out by rows of tall spruce trees. A gentle breeze was blowing carrying along the scent of hundreds of lilies of the valley that appeared to grow wild along that side of house. They didn't, of course, but the small bed planted by a previous owner had expanded across the yard to form a blanket of green capped by clusters of fragrant, bell-shaped white flowers.

It was good to be home; that is, what had once been my home. It was quiet out here in the country, although Plainview hadn't really been that noisy. The house was set back from the road so the traffic wasn't too disturbing, although in the dark of a winter's night, when the air was clear and sounds carried, I was sometimes sure the big trucks that passed were on the front porch. The spruce and maple trees----some of them nearly one hundred years old and giants----that surrounded the place cooled the house in summer and sheltered it from winter's cold and icy winds.

We talked about a lot of things, but always came back to Rory and his murder. In a move to change the subject to something lighter, I asked, "Have you been involved in any more bank robberies?"

"No, we haven't had one since Great Valley ten years ago. I guess the guys who were doing them have moved to greener pastures. After all, the banks in these mountains are few and far between and probably don't keep near as much cash on hand at those down in Kingston or up in Albany."

I got a quizzical look an my face. "What do you mean, guys? I thought the conclusion was both robberies had been done by the same person. Singular, that is."

In an annoyed tone, my mother put things straight. "Shows how much they know. Common sense says at least two people were involved, but once they made up their mind, common sense went out the window."

"Well, sheriff," I laughed. "Explain your theory to me, maybe I'll have more sense than the official force."

"Probably only one person did the first robbery, the one in Plainview, but it took two to pull off the one in Great Valley. Remember they found the getaway car behind that old house at the end of the road up on the ridge? Then they figured the robber went over the mountain on a motorcycle that had been stashed there. Remember that?"

Yes, I remembered that. Had my mother been reading too many crime novels? Here she was talking about pulling off a robbery, getaway cars, and stashing vehicles in out-of-the-way locations.

She hardly paused, however, "Well, just how do think the motorcycle got there in the first place? It was too big to have fitted in the trunk of the car and it certainly didn't drive there all by itself. And how do suppose the robber got to Catskill to start with? He had to have someone drive him there so he could steal the car and then to pick him up after he hid the motorcycle behind the house. I suppose he could have hitchhiked, but not too much traffic uses that dead-end road; in fact, I don't think too many cars use the road over the ridge on any regular basis. A hitchhiker up there would be something most people would remember."

With that she shoved back her chair, went into the kitchen, and returned in a few minutes with two dishes, each holding a brownie covered with vanilla ice cream topped by hot fudge sauce. Another of my favorite things. Mothers are great; yes, they are.

Her analysis was right, of course. I just hadn't thought it through the way she had. On the other hand, I hadn't had a front-row seat when these earthshaking events (and they were that to the folks on the Mountain Top) had occurred.

I took my things upstairs to my old room. It was the same, but it wasn't. The furniture was different. Over time, most of that from my days of occupancy had found its way to my own home and was now in Emma's room. At first, she wasn't sure she wanted her room fitted out with antiques, as she called my treasured pieces, but she and they came to accept each other. But a gentle breeze came through the open windows and stirred the limbs of the big spruce tree outside so the tips of them scraped the tin roof of the porch just below. In my first nights in this room long ago, that scraping noise had terrified me; I envisioned creepy crawling things lurking just outside the window. I came to appreciate the comfort of the sound, however, and sometimes thought I could detect a musical tone in it as I drifted off to sleep.

I reveled in the calm security of the old house and my mother's presence the days I was there even though she was in and out tending to her many interests. She was usually gone when I, generally a late riser, came down in the morning, but she returned at noon so we could have lunch and talk together. However, I couldn't overcome the disquiet I felt when alone. I had the feeling something had yet to happen and I was still a player in the game, whatever game it was. I assumed the investigation of Rory's murder was continuing, but I really didn't want to know about it. As long as I wasn't being hauled in for another round of questioning, I was willing to leave the detecting to those who were charged to carry it out.

I did feel I still owed something to Rory even though he was gone. We had made plans for a hike together and decided to go ahead with it as sort of a remembrance to him. So it was that when Monday morning dawned bright and sunny and cool, I announced to my mother I'd be gone for the day, off on a hike of some of the trails near North Lake.

She was completely taken aback at this. "Ellyn, you never go hiking. Too bad your father isn't here for this one. He'd never believe it."

I explained my reason, but it didn't make a whole lot of sense when I tried to put it into words. But mothers are mothers first of all. "Let me put up a lunch for you," she said, as I made ready to leave.

I stopped in Plainview on the way. I wanted some heavier socks and expected to find what I needed in Simon's Clothing on Main Street across and a couple doors up from the tattoo parlor. As I returned to my car after making my purchase, Wing came over. She called my name and, as she approached, I saw she was holding a white envelope in one hand. She handed it to me.

"Some years ago," she explained, "Rory gave me this. He wanted me to keep it in a safe place and to tell no one, even Mack, about it. If something happened to him, he said I should give it to you. I didn't know who you were then, but he said you'd show up when that time came, if it came. I don't know what's in the envelope; in fact, it was so long ago, I had almost forgotten about it. But for the last few days I have had this feeling I was supposed to do something. This morning I suddenly remembered and dug it out from the bottom of the strong box where I keep what few important papers I have."

We stood facing each other for a minute or two, saying nothing. I noticed a tear roll down her weathered cheek. She wiped it away, turned on the heel of her boot, crossed the street, and entered the front door of the tattoo parlor. She didn't look back.

I was more than a little surprised, stunned, perhaps. I wondered what it was Rory had thought so important to put down on paper so long ago. What did he want me to know? Why me? I wondered how many times I had asked myself that question over the last week or so. Well, I wasn't going to open the envelope there in the middle of Main Street. I decided to wait till I reached some quiet, sunny spot along one of the trails. That would be far more appropriate considering Rory's love of the outdoors. I put the envelope in the small pack my mother had given me to carry my lunch. It was one my brother had when he was a teenager, she told me. It had hung in the cellar since then, she said, and I might just as well get some use out of it. She was sure he had forgotten all about it, anyway.

The Smoky Bear girl wasn't at the gate house, her place being taken that day by a male of the species, also ridiculously young. Since I was the only one arriving at the moment (Mondays were usually a slow day, the young man told me), he was willing to take some time to help me select the route for my hike. Not too long, I told him, but long enough to be meaningful, and I also didn't want a lot of ups and downs. Using a trail map he marked out a hike (he called it a walk) of about two miles that would bring me back to the gate house. I could leave my car in the nearby parking lot, he said, and the circle route he suggested would return me to it in good time. Along the way I would pass near the top of Kaaterskill Falls and I did look forward to seeing that natural wonder at long last.

The first part of the route took me along the campsite road that dropped down to the outlet of South Lake. Beyond that I followed the winding trail that climbed South Mountain to a junction with the blue-marked trail I was to follow to the falls. Just past the bend in the trail where a red-marked trail joined, was the site of the old Hotel Kaaterskill. This massive hostelry, built in 1881 to rival the Catskill Mountain House, burned to the ground in the late summer of 1924. I stayed on the blue trail (being glad I wasn't color blind) which wound down to the top of the ledgy escarpment that looked into the deep Kaaterskill Clove formed by the Kaaterskill Creek, that had, over millennia, carved a passage through the rock on its way to the Hudson River off in the distance. I passed a couple of lookouts with the picturesque names of Inspiration Point and Sunset Rock, so my map informed me.

Near a wide turn to the right, I stopped to read the inscription of the Layman Monument. Near here, it said, Frank D. Layman, a local man, had lost his life on August 10, 1900, while helping to fight a forest fire.

I could hear the thunder of the falls not far ahead. As I came close to them, the trail turned left to drop steeply along the stream to eventually reach Route 23A far below. The falls are a magnificent spectacle, world-renowned and historic, captured in numerous paintings by Thomas Cole and others of the Hudson River School of Landscape Painting. They are reputed to be the highest in the country easterly of the Mississippi River dropping in two cascades, the first a sheer fall of 166 feet and the second a 64-foot tumble of water over a massive ledge. A large sweeping cavern circles nearly 300 feet in back of the first fall and one can scrabble along it to look out through the stream of water as it plunges downward in a fine misty spray. I didn't attempt the gymnastics required for that view. It is said that during particularly cold winters the upper fall freezes into sort of a tube reaching from the frozen pool at the bottom to the lip of the cliff above while the water continues to flow within it.

I climbed the trail to a point at the top and picked out what looked like a comfortable spot next to a large rock not far from the stream. I put my pack on the ground, took out the lunch my mother had prepared, and settled down, leaning my back against the rock. As I munched on my sandwich, I opened the envelope and started to read the message Rory had left for me.

ELEVEN

Dear El,

If you are reading this, it's because I'm no longer around to tell my story in person. If something happens, I know you'll come to see me off to wherever it is failures are sent when they depart this world. Of all the people I have known in my checkered life, you were the most sincere, thoughtful, and caring. You always seemed ready to accept me as I was and to listen patiently to the tales of woe I burdened you with from time to time. Of course, others also accepted me for what I was, but made it quite obvious they didn't care for what that was. You were the only true friend I ever had and, as poor compensation for that, you'll have to listen to the saddest tale of all.

You must have heard about the bank robbery we had here in Plainview. I'm sure it didn't make the national papers, but I know Dr. Jan keeps you up to date on local events and it certainly was one of those.

It was in the summer of 1978. The whole thing was well-planned. An alarm was called in reporting a terrible automobile accident down the Clove. Nearly everyone in town responded—those who should have and those who wanted to see for themselves just how bad it was. I heard the siren on the firehouse, followed in a few minutes by those on the trucks heading down the mountain. I was fishing in Gooseberry Creek out back of the village over near the cemetery and didn't know what was going on. I didn't belong to the fire company and wouldn't have gone otherwise even if I had been in town.

In a little while, I heard someone coming along the path that runs through the woods by the creek. I was behind some trees and shrubs, but could see the path clearly. The person was running. He carried some kind of bag and was wearing a ski mask that completely covered his head, except for openings around his eyes and nose. He pulled it off as he went by. It was Jamie Timmerman. Obviously, he hadn't seen me. He ran on and soon I heard a car start and then fade away as it went up Bloomer Road toward the Elka Park Road. I hadn't noticed the car, so figured it had been pulled into the old woods road down near the bridge where it would be hidden from those who passed on the main road.

It wasn't until I went to Warm's for supper that I heard what had happened. I didn't know what to do. Who would believe me? Here I was, a convict, not too well thought of by anyone. Who would take my word over that of Jamie, a prominent local businessman from one of the oldest families in town? Someone would be sure to point out I hadn't been at the scene of the supposed accident and must have been in town when the robbery had taken place. I just knew I would be the one they would pin it on. I decided not to tell what I had seen.

A couple of years later, one night when I had too much to drink, Jamie came in Curran's Tavern and sat next to me. We were down at the end of the bar out of the range of anyone's hearing. The few who were there were watching a baseball game on television and not paying any attention to us. I don't know why I did it, the drink, I suppose, but I told him where I had been that day and about seeing him on the path.

He looked at me curiously for a few minutes and said nothing. When he did speak, it filled me with dread. "Keeping quiet about this for so long and not notifying the police has kind of put you in a box, old friend."

I didn't know what he meant, but as he explained it, I had impeded justice and become sort of an accessory by being silent. "If you tell now, with your record, you'd probably end up back in jail."

Maybe he was right but, even if not, who'd believe me now any more than when it all had happened. I couldn't have taken that, El. Those years in jail were the worst I ever spent. My cell was so small, I could hardly move around. I couldn't see out. When we were allowed outside, it was in an area surrounded by high concrete walls. I couldn't see a tree, or hear the birds sing, or see fish jumping in a stream. It was just me and the sky overhead. I couldn't risk going back to that, so I kept quiet.

Jamie and I saw one another in the years that followed, but we hardly spoke. We didn't really avoid each other, but kept distance between us. Until the spring of 1983, that is. I was surprised when he stopped me on the street one day. He was going to buy a bike—a motorcycle to you—and wanted me to help him pick it out. I was the only person he knew who was any kind of an authority on bikes and he wanted to be sure he ended up with the right one, he said. It sounded all right to me so I agreed to help. He was looking for something that would be suitable for highway driving, he said, but could also be used on back roads and trails through the woods. We shopped around and he finally selected one. He hadn't ridden bikes before, so I kind of coached him the first few times he rode. After that, we went on some rides together. We seemed to have forgotten the difficulty between us. At least that's what I thought.

On a ride near the end of May, we drove to Mountain Water and up the road that goes over the ridge. About halfway along, Jamie, who was out ahead, turned into a single-lane road. This was new country to me and it wasn't till later I found out it was called Condon Hollow and was the beginning of an old road that went over the mountain and down Turk Hollow in Halcott. It didn't appear to have been used for a long time being covered with grass and weeds. Limbs reaching out from the trees on each side of the road pretty much closed it in. After about half a mile we came to a house at what appeared to be the end of the road. The house had been lived in once, I suppose, but that had been some time before. Some of the windows were broken, the paint had peeled in long strips all around, and the front door hung loose on broken hinges.

Jamie pulled his bike around back. A single-car garage was in the back of the house under a porch that led out from what looked like a kitchen. The door to the garage slid on small metal wheels along a track on the top. Jamie easily opened it. I realized the track and wheels had been oiled not long before. He wheeled his bike inside and closed the door.

I had no idea what was going on. "What are you doing?" I asked. "Oh, I rented this place for the summer," he said. "I'm going to leave my bike here for a while. I'll drive the car over now and then and take the bike on rides over the roads in the mountains around here. I'll hop on back of your bike now and you can take me back to Plainview."

It sounded kind of dumb to me, but I didn't say so. We rode to Plainview and I thought that was the end of it. It wasn't. A week or so later, Jamie asked me to give him a ride to Catskill and I did. He said he had some business to attend to in the court house and I let him off there. I asked where and when I was to pick him up and he said not to worry about that, he had a ride home with someone who was coming along later. A couple of days after that, I saw him ride his bike up Main Street and figured he must have had someone else take him over to Mountain Water to pick it up. He waved to me as he went by and I thought no more of it.

Soon after that the bank in Great Valley was robbed. The way it happened was a lot like the robbery in Plainview. The police felt the two were connected and probably had been done by the same person. I thought so too, but unlike the police, had more than a suspicion who it was. I decided to do some investigation on my own, but waited till things quieted down a bit. I saw Jamie on his bike a number of times in between.

It wasn't until early fall when I felt I could chance a trip back to that old abandoned house. The dirt road leading in to it looked the same except through one wet spot, I saw a tire track, not from a bike, but from a car. I rode around back of the house and found a green Ford sedan parked under the overhanging porch. I opened the garage door and looked inside. It was empty. As I stood there looking at the car, I suddenly realized I was more than an accessory after the fact. I was an accomplice this time. Jamie's friendship had been well calculated; he had drawn me deeply within his web of deceit. If before I had questioned whether I could be sent to jail for not telling the authorities what I knew, I had no doubt where I would now end up.

I carried my guilt and secret around for weeks, for months. I really did avoid Jamie although I couldn't help but see him now and then. He always waved as he went by on his bike and I waved back, but only because others would wonder if I didn't. I seemed to see Chris Rafferty wherever I went and was sure each time he was ready to haul me off to the county jail. I might just as well have been in jail, I guess. I all but gave up the carefree life I had enjoyed before.

Then came Lorna. You would have liked her, El. She was kind like you. She liked me not for what I was, but for who I was. She rode bikes, too. In fact, we met at a rally up near Albany. We started going on rides together and, finally, she came to Plainview and moved into my apartment up over Wing's place. We were going to get married. I told her about my troubles with the law and my jail term, none of that bothered her. That was in the past she said, and I should leave it there. I also told her about Jamie and the bank robberies and my part in the second one. That was my mistake. It really irritated her and one day she confronted him with what she knew. That was her mistake.

She had a job under the mountain and rode her bike to and from it every day no matter what the weather. She was a good rider. One day not long after the incident with Jamie, she didn't make it. When she didn't come home that night, I called Chris. He checked at the place where she worked. She hadn't come in that day and hadn't called to say she wouldn't be at work, which was unusual, the folks she worked for said.

We found her and the bike the next morning. She was down the steep embankment on the right side of the road a little way up from the lookout and parking area above the hairpin turn. She was dead. Her head was battered from where it had hit on a rock and the rest of her body was scraped and bruised from the fall down the rough slope. The bike was farther down. I climbed down to it. It was pretty well beat up too, but I found some marks on the back fender that looked like they had been made by the bumper of a small truck or a car. I figured someone had run up behind her and, when he came too close, she had tried to outrun him and wasn't able to. The vehicle had only to nudge the back of the bike to throw it out of control at that speed. She and the bike had flipped over the guardrail and onto the rocks below. The police investigation concluded much the same thing. The truck was never found.

Naturally, I was sure Jamie had done it, but couldn't prove it. Of course, I couldn't pass on my suspicions to the police without explaining why I thought he had done it. I did look over the bumper of the hardware store's truck the next time I saw it parked on the street, but didn't see any marks or paint on it that would match the fender of the bike. However, the impact would have been slight and might not have left any sign. Also, the hardware store probably carried some kind of metal cleaner that could take off marks and paint such as that anyway.

There it was then, El. My chance for a happy life was gone in an instant. I knew why and who, but could do nothing about it. I suppose I should have turned him in and accepted the consequences. The one person who brought smiles to me was gone and I wasn't interested in finding another to take her place. Such a person didn't exist. Lorna had been the proverbial one of a kind as far as I was concerned. I drew further into myself and shunned people, places, and things. In effect, I became a hermit, going out only to work with Mack. Wing fixed my lunch each day and did my grocery shopping so I could make other meals for myself.

As I write this, it's six months since Lorna's death—or murder really. I decided to put this all down on paper in case something happens to me. I consider what Jamie did to Lorna as a warning for me to keep quiet. Maybe I'm even living on borrowed time. I will give this letter to Wing for safekeeping. She is a good person, no matter what else you may hear. You will like her, El, when the two of you meet. She will like you, I'm sure.

So, that's it. I'm sorry to shift my burden to your shoulders, but I know you will not refuse it. Think kindly of me.

Your friend,
Rory Hale.

TWELVE

TO SAY I WAS ASTOUNDED would be but to belittle the word. I'm not sure what I was, but it wasn't happy. I sat there dumfounded (even that hardly states my feelings of the moment) not realizing or paying attention to the fact that a colony of ants were making every effort to carry off the half-eaten sandwich I had dropped on the ground. I leafed through the pages of Rory's letter hoping, I suppose, it wasn't true or was written in disappearing ink with the words soon to fade from the paper. They didn't. I picked up the aluminum foil that had been the wrapping of my sandwich and put it in my pack. I left what remained of the sandwich for the ants. I arranged the pages of the letter in order, folded and put them back in the envelope. What should I do next? How I wished Rory had also written some suggestion about what he wanted me to do with what I now knew. Or better yet, that he was still here so we could discuss it. He wasn't, of course. I was on my own.

I put the envelope in the pocket on the front of the pack. As I was snapping it shut, I sensed something, someone, near by. I looked up the trail in back of the rock. Jamie stood there. How long he had been watching me I don't know. I tried to be casual.

"Hi, fancy meeting you here. You must have decided to use this fine day for a hike just like I did."

It didn't work. "What were you reading?" he asked.

154

"Oh, just some letters from home. From my daughter and my husband. I brought them along to read over again while I was eating my lunch." I had a feeling that wasn't going to work either. It didn't.

"I thought maybe it was whatever was in that envelope Wing gave you back in town."

So he had seen us on the street. I should have known that. After all, the hardware store is only a few doors away from where I had parked my car and the whole street is visible from the store's big front windows. He must have followed me and, seeing the Buick in the parking area just up from the gate house, asked Smoky Bear if he knew what trail I was walking. And that young person, under orders to be helpful and courteous to the public, had told him. In the few seconds it took to run that through my mind, I finished closing the flap and slung the pack on my back.

"I think I should have a look at your letter," Jamie continued.

"No, Jamie. I can't do that. It's a personal note to me and not something to share."

I knew I wouldn't be able to prevent him from taking the envelope should he decide to. The tone of his voice and the look on his face said he was about ready to make a move in that direction. I looked around for an escape route. I was no runner and, in fact, may be the only person in the class who got a failing mark in physical education every quarter it was a required subject. I was even less athletic now, my knees creaked even when I walked or climbed stairs. Nevertheless, I had to make an attempt. I ran as fast as I could down the slope toward the stream, my abrupt move being enough of a surprise to give me a head start.

The stream ahead, running in spate from the heavy rain the day before, presented a major obstacle. I was no more a jumper than a runner. The only leap anyone had ever known me to make had been years ago when I was an early teen-ager. My brother and I were walking through the cemetery across the road from our house in Mountain Water. We were startled to see a snake, at least twenty feet long in my eyes, but probably no more than three. Still long enough to me. My brother didn't hold the same fear of reptiles as I, so I left him behind. I ran toward our house and easily hurdled the cemetery fence. My mother, hearing my screams, had come to the front door to see what was the matter and saw the whole thing. She still occasionally mentions the event and how she wished she had had a camera to take a picture of my Olympic-style steeplechase.

I jumped and cleared the stream in a single bound. My right knee nearly gave way as I landed and I almost fell. I recovered quickly and ran up the trail toward the gate house. I heard a yell and a splash behind me. I looked over my shoulder to see what had happened. Jamie was in the water; he must have slipped or stumbled as he, too, tried to jump the stream. He was desperately trying to regain his footing, but the rock ledge that formed the bed of the stream, worn smooth and slippery by millions of years of flowing water, gave no purchase. He was swept along.

"Help, El. Help," he called, but I could do nothing to help him, nor could anyone else.

He shot over the edge of the cliff. His cries turned to screams. I put my hands over my ears, but could still hear them. Then, they stopped. No other sound interrupted the rush and roar of the water. I was stunned; struck mute by what I had seen. I couldn't bring myself to look over the edge of the cliff. I turned and hurried on toward the gate house.

The young Smoky Bear person saw me coming and greeted me as I appeared. "Hi, did your friend find you?"

That was just too much. I broke down in sobs. He knew not what was wrong, but gently took my elbow, guided me into the little gate house, and sat me on a stool in the corner. After a minute or two I recovered enough to blurt out my story. Immediately, he turned from sympathy to efficiency. He first called his supervisor at the campsite, then the local forest ranger, the rescue squad, and, at my urgent request, Chris Rafferty. It wasn't long before the campsite person came and whisked me off to his headquarters cabin, leaving word with the gate house attendant to direct law enforcement there when they arrived. As I left, I thanked the young man for his kindness; I had, perhaps, been wrong in characterizing him as a Smoky Bear clone.

The campsite caretaker pointed me to a cushioned rocking chair in the living room of the cabin and thoughtfully fixed me a cup of tea. As I drank it, I could hear sirens approaching and then fading.

"That's the rescue squad," he explained. "They've turned down the old Laurel House Road. That will take them to the top of the falls. They'll have quite a scramble to get to the bottom." A car slid to a stop out front. Chris burst through the door. "My God, El, what happened?"

I opened the pocket on the front of my pack and took out the envelope. "Here, you'd better read this. It's from Rory," I said, handing it to him. Chris opened the envelope and started to read. He hadn't got past the first page, when he decided to sit down. Pulling a chair out from the nearby table, he continued, shaking his head and mumbling curse words to himself as he read page after page. When he reached the end, he came over and hugged me long and hard. We each shed a tear or two on the other's shoulder----except my tears went on the front of his jacket; I still couldn't reach his shoulder.

A car, two cars, pulled up outside. The door opened and Jan and the sheriff came in. Handing the letter to her, Chris said, "Read this before you say much of anything. The sheriff and I'll go down to the falls. I'll explain things to him as we go."

Jan's reaction to the letter was about the same as Chris's. She read slowly as if trying to comprehend it all. Finally, she said, "What a sad thing. What a sad thing." Over and over she said it, shaking her head in disbelief as she did.

Retrieving Jamie's body was a gruesome business. Those who were there said it had been shattered by the concussion from the long drop over the lip of the cliff to the pool of water far below. Then it had been beaten against the rocks on the shore of the pool as the eddies and currents washed it back and forth and round and round. Spatters of blood marked the rocks here and there tracking the tortuous path it had followed. Once they had him loaded on the stretcher, it was a struggle to maneuver it up the precipitous slopes that ringed the cirque of the falls. The stretcher bearers slipped and slid as they climbed, clutching at tree roots, rocks, and anything else that appeared to offer a hold. More than once they nearly lost the stretcher and the sad burden it held.

Chris and the sheriff returned as we heard the sirens of the rescue squad vehicles making their way toward Plainview. Sheriff Branson still looked like a grandfather to me, and I guess that's just what I needed. He patted me softly on the shoulder with his big, beefy hands. "There, there, Missy, you've had a bit of a fright. Don't you fret none. We can get along without bothering you for a day or two. We'll need to take that letter with us. You run along with the doctor here. She'll take good care of you."

As much as I would have liked the comfort of Jan's house, I really wanted to go home. Not to Georgia and Cal's Corner, not quite yet. Home to Mountain Water, to that big, old house, and my own room. I wanted to hear the wind sough through the spruce tree and the brush of its branches on the metal roof.

Jan had already called my mother so she was expecting us. The table was set on the inside/outside porch. It was tomato soup and egg salad sandwiches again. We didn't talk much as we ate. Quiet companionship seemed to be the best medicine for each of us. As we finished, Chris Rafferty pulled up in my car. My mother couldn't persuade him to sit a while and have something to eat. He was all business and that was comforting. He and Jan then left in her car. I climbed the stairs to my room and lay on the soft bed. The breeze blew softly through the open window. I drifted off to sleep, a troubled sleep, but a welcome sleep nonetheless.

I didn't hear the telephone ring when Roger and Emma called. Jan had called them earlier to tell them the story of my ordeal. My mother said she thought it best if I was left to sleep and would call them back when I awoke. She assured them I was weathering the storm in good order. No, she didn't think it necessary for them to come; it was only a few days before I would be home anyway and it was more important for them to be there waiting when I stepped off the plane.

The sheriff and trusty Officer Felton came the next day. This time around it was more a social visit than a session of questions and answers. They were, in the words of Joe Friday, interested in just the facts. The sheriff returned the letter—he had made copies for his records and other law enforcement units. "It's a personal thing and yours alone. It must have been of some comfort to him to know he had a friend like you," he said, with a kindly smile.

I had always marveled at the speed and reliability of the information network of the Mountain Top. No matter what the news—good, bad, or indifferent—literally everyone knew about it quickly and at the same time. So it was with this. The telephone rang all that day with people calling to see how I was and if they could help me or my mother in any way. Folks I hadn't seen in years dropped in bringing a pie, a salad, a batch of cookies, and a few tomatoes, fresh-picked from someone's little greenhouse. Soon the refrigerator was full and the kitchen table "runneth over." They were a funny bunch, these mountain people. They left you alone most of the time—what you did with your life was your own business. But if they thought your spirits needed a lift, they showed up in numbers as if nothing had happened.

Of course, the funeral followed in a couple of days. The casket was closed, as good as the local undertaker was, he couldn't repair the damage of a 166-foot fall and beatings against the hard rocks of the Catskills. As before, Jan, my mother, and I went together. The funeral parlor wasn't nearly as full as when we had gathered for Rory just a few short days ago. Those of the Class of '68 who had gone to homes far away didn't return. The bikers weren't there either. I felt sorry for Jamie's wife; the anguish on her face clearly indicated she hadn't known of his alter ego and other life. She seemed to be asking forgiveness on Jamie's behalf for something that wasn't her fault.

He was buried in the same quiet cemetery, but on the side away from Rory's plot. I made my way to the family after the grave-side service and offered my sympathy saying I would always remember the good times Jamie and I had together when we were in school. It was an awkward moment for them and for me and, although they knew I was sincere, we were all glad when it was over.

I was going to spend my last two nights at Jan's house, so late the next afternoon I took leave from my mother and the old, big, comfortable farmhouse. While we were glad to have had these days together, we had obviously hoped for a more tranquil time. As I left, I assured her all three of us would be up for a week—no, two weeks—over Christmas. I meant it, and she knew I did. It made our parting a little easier than it might have been.

THIRTEEN

I WAS SO TIRED I slept until nearly ten. I guess everything caught up with me all at once. I felt guilty (well, just a little), because I knew Jan had been seeing patients since eight. I would be leaving next morning, so had planned to spend the day driving around looking at places important to my younger years and engraving the sight of them on my memory screen. And, thinking.

Coming out of the shower, I discovered a cup of coffee and a buttered muffin on the night table. Jan must have taken time between patients to put them there. She also left a note written on a prescription form. "Good morning, Sleepy. I have a heavy afternoon, so probably won't have time to talk. I'll see you when I'm through saving lives."

I spent the day pretty much as planned, not returning until the middle of the afternoon. I went onto the patio and stretched out on the window seat with the magazines that had come in Jan's mail that day: *Newsweek*, *The New Yorker*, *Rolling Stone*, and *Medical Economics*—about as eclectic a selection as one could devise. I really wasn't interested in reading. I just wanted to sit, peacefully, and pretend life was normal. I was having a hard time making sense of all that had happened during the past couple of weeks. I doubted any of it had made *Newsweek*, but looked anyway—it hadn't. I got up and walked around the room, straightened the blinds, flicked some dust off a table. I settled on the love seat and flipped through *The New Yorker*, reading only the cartoons.

The swinging door to the kitchen opened and Jan backed through it. She was carrying a tray brimming with cheese, crackers, grapes, and two glasses of wine. She set it on the small, low table and herself into the lounging chair. As she sipped her wine, she leaned her head back and closed her eyes. "I have never been so tired in my entire life and that includes medical school."

She leaned forward to pick up a piece of cheese. "This whole experience seems just a little bit too surreal. I mean, these things don't happen to people we know." She smiled. "That sounds like something my mother would have said. But truly? A murder, two old unsolved crimes, mystery, intrigue, another death. Who would have thought it?"

"Oh, by the way," she went on. "Chris asked me to tell you the story of the key."

"Oh, no! Not the key again."

"Yes, the key. The one you walked off with. All these years, Rory and Wing and anyone else who might have had reason to know thought just one key existed. Rory had destroyed any extras. He was a very private person when it came to his place and his things and didn't want people snooping around where they didn't belong. Or, so we thought. Now we know he had another reason—he was protecting himself. Well, of course, it didn't work. As it turns out, Jamie had a duplicate key. He must have taken the brand and number of the lock some time when Rory was away or at work and then made a key at the hardware store. Chris said they found it in an envelope in the back of the cash register drawer."

I looked out on the back yard. A kid was running across the grass, chasing a baseball. A little girl sat on the steps of the house across the street, playing jacks. Everything looked serene, calm, and all in order as I remembered our old world to be.

"Have you thought?" I asked, "That it seems like none of these things really happened? Sometimes I think I'm going to wake up and realize I saw this on television or in the movies." I selected a piece of

Havarti. "It really does seem more like something you would read in a book."

Jan looked at me for a minute. "I think you're right. Why don't you go home and write about it? You always used to be writing things years ago."

"If I did, what would I call it? 'Things Not to Do at Your High School Reunion'?"

"No. How about 'Reasons Not to Go to Your High School Reunion'?"

"Maybe I'll call it, 'Why You Should Never Go to Any Reunion.' Now there's one thing I am sure of. When the 50th comes around, don't save that room down the hall for me, because I'm not coming."

My best friend and I laughed for the first time in many days.

A Closing Note
To The Reader

WHEN OUR DAUGHTER died suddenly nearly three years ago, she left a void in our lives that can never be filled. She also left the manuscript of a murder mystery she had been working on. It was based, in part, on the 20th high school reunion she had attended a few years earlier. Although a murder hadn't then occurred, she used the experience of seeing friends and visiting places from the past as a theme on which to create a fictional story of that time.

I have edited her manuscript and, hopefully, rounded off some of the rough edges that inevitably mark the first draft of any book. As I did, I recognized some of the characters she portrayed, while others remained strangers, as the saying goes, to protect the innocent. Many of the scenes and incidents she wrote about and wove into the narrative are real although some have been altered by either name, date, or otherwise to better blend into the story being told.

Airilee was a voracious reader. She was the only person I ever knew who could---and did---read two, three, and more books at the same time. She kept one in every room in the house that she frequented on a regular basis. She would pick up each book as she passed by and read a few pages before putting it down and going on to the next room and book. She even read in the bathtub although this practice once came to grief. She fell asleep and dropped the book into the water. She awoke to find loose pages floating all around her—*Auntie Mame*, by Patrick Dennis, nearly drowned. Undeterred, she dried the pages by spreading them on towels, put them back in order, and finished reading the book.

With such love for the printed word, it is not surprising she harbored a yen to write herself and did. However, she suffered a trait that was, one might say, unbecoming to a writer. She didn't want anyone, other than her mother and one or two close friends, to read what she had written. "It isn't good enough, " she'd say. I hope she feels differently about *Class of '68* and, also, that those who read it do too.

Murder in the Shawangunks takes Ward Eastman into new territory. The tale told here is one that has been taking shape in my mind for some time. As I finished editing Airilee's book, I decided to give Ward one more shot at running a culprit to ground and to use his adventure as a companion piece to the *Class of '68*.

It is, however, his last foray into the field of detection. His remaining days out on the transit line are few and the time will soon come for him to really retire. On the other hand, who knows what evil lurks in the minds of men and if a body may yet lie hidden in some nook or cranny of the Shawangunks or his beloved Catskills just waiting for him to stumble across it?

Norman J. Van Valkenburgh
Saugerties, New York

December 17, 1998

Other Ward Eastman mysteries you will enjoy:

Murder in the Catskills

Ward Eastman finds a skeleton in rugged terrain near the hamlet of South Branch. From the moment he starts to unravel the mystery, Eastman finds himself enmeshed amid layers of genealogy, history, and topography.

Mayhem in the Catskills

While surveying a large estate in the central Catskills, Ward Eastman discovers the body of the recently murdered owner in a remote cabin. All doors and windows are locked and soon there are too many suspects.

Mischief in the Catskills

A deer hunter is lost in a blinding blizzard. Eastman and his surveying crew are joined by law enforcement officials and volunteers as the search intensifies. But was the hunter really lost? A mystery novella with five masterful short stories.

About the author

Norman J. Van Valkenburgh was born in West Kill in Greene County and has spent most of his life in or in sight of the Catskill Mountains. He is a licensed surveyor and 32-year veteran of the New York State Department of Environmental Conservation.

About the publisher

Purple Mountain Press, founded in 1973, is a publishing company committed to producing the best original books of regional interest as well as bringing back into print significant older works. For a free catalog of more than 300 hard-to-find books about New York State, write Purple Mountain Press, Ltd., P.O. Box E3, Fleischmanns, New York 12430-0378, or call 914-254-4062, or fax 914-254-4476, or email Purple@catskill.net. Website: http://www.catskill.net/purple